RESCUED BY A VISCOUNT

REGENCY RAKES SERIES

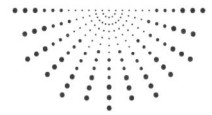

WENDY VELLA

Rescued By A Viscount is a work of fiction. Names, places, and incidents either are products of the author's imagination or are used fictitiously.

Rescued By A Viscount published by Wendy Vella

Copyright © 2014 Wendy Vella

OTHER BOOKS BY WENDY VELLA

HISTORICAL ROMANCE

Regency Rakes Series

Duchess By Chance

Rescued By A Viscount

Tempting Miss Allender

The Langley Sisters Series

Lady In Disguise

Lady In Demand

Lady In Distress

The Lady Plays Her Ace

The Lady Seals Her Fate

The Lady's Dangerous Love

Lords Of Night Street Series

Lord Gallant

Lord Valiant

Lord Valorous

Lord Noble

Sinclair and Raven Series

Sensing Danger

Seeing Danger

Touched By Danger

Scent Of Danger

Vision Of Danger

The Haddon Brothers Series

The Earl's Encounter

Stand Alone Titles

Christmas Wishes

The Reluctant Countess

Mistletoe And The Marquess

CONTEMPORARY ROMANCE

The Lake Howling Series

A Promise Of Home

The Texan Meets His Match

How Sweet It Is

It Only Took You

Don't Look Back

A Long Way Home

Ryker Falls Series

Somebody To Love

From This Moment

Love Me Tender

To Sophie and Nate.

*I may not be perfect
but when I look at my children
I know I got something perfectly right.
So proud of you both.
Love you xx*

CHAPTER ONE

*V*iscount Kelkirk ran down the narrow lane and past the shops, his long legs covering the distance with ease. "Minerva's Miracle Cures," he muttered, glancing at the sign above one of the shop fronts. As if crushed eye of newt and several cloves of garlic with a pinch of the ridiculous could cure anything. Put a label on something and call it the elixir of life and desperate and foolish people tended to buy it.

Skirting two boys playing in a puddle, he increased his pace, thinking of the horse he was going to buy if he made it to the rendezvous with Daniel in time. At the end of the shops, he turned right and ran into someone coming the other way. Catching the body as she cried out, he staggered until his back collided with a wall. The air expelled from his lungs in a loud whoosh. Wrapping his arms around the woman as she tripped on his feet, Simon pulled her into his chest until she steadied.

"Please accept my apologies, madam. Are you unhurt?" he said as he fought for breath.

"Forgive me, sir—in my haste, I did not see you coming."

He knew that voice.

"Claire?"

"Dear god!" She stumbled back a few paces, staring at him, her brown eyes wide, expression stricken.

"What's wrong?" Simon said, advancing, which made her scurry further backward. "Claire, why are you here alone… dressed like that?" he added, looking at her worn black coat and bonnet. Searching around them, he saw no sign of a maid or anyone who should be accompanying her. His eyes narrowed as they returned to her and took in her shabby appearance. Claire Belmont was never anything but elegantly attired. Every item she donned showcased the beauty of her soft cream skin, strawberry blonde curls, and lush body, yet dressed in that, she could have passed for a servant.

"I…uh, have to go."

She was pale and scared; fear announced itself in every line of her face and the rigid way she held her body. She was looking everywhere but at him, almost as if she was searching for someone.

"Who are you looking for?

Her eyes quickly returned to his, the brown depths wary.

"I must leave at once, Lord Kelkirk. Please excuse me."

"If you think I'll let you walk about here unescorted in a distressed state, then think again," Simon reached for her arm as she prepared to leave, but she evaded him and then, to his stunned surprise, she picked up her skirts and ran. "Claire!" She didn't stop as he roared her name, and in seconds, he was following. She was fast—he'd give her that—but he was bigger and his stride longer, and he was soon gaining on her. She turned briefly to see how close he was, and that gave him the opportunity he needed.

"Claire, stop." He grabbed her arm, but she swung her reticule, and whatever was inside connected with his jaw, sending him stumbling backward. She didn't pause as he cursed, and in seconds, had fled. Simon waited until his ears stopped ringing and then followed. Once out of the lane, he looked up and down the street. There were plenty of carriages and hackneys but no sign of Claire. She could be inside one, but he had no hope of catching them and opening each to look. Slowly retracing his steps to where she'd collided with him, he looked down the narrow lane. Why was she here dressed in old clothes, and what the hell had the haughty Claire Belmont so upset that she would run from him like that?

He had known her for two years, since their best friends had married, but their relationship was not what one would term close. For the most, they rubbed along with each other, however when he was with Lady Claire Belmont, Simon always felt as though someone was jabbing him repeatedly in the side with a dull edged instrument. It was a nasty, irritating feeling he had never been able to dislodge. She wasn't like other women, who seemed more than happy to like him. Claire challenged him constantly. She said he needed provocation, as most women just gazed at him adoringly. Of course he provoked her back, because there was nothing quite as enticing as seeing Claire Belmont ruffled, her usually immaculate feathers standing on end.

His eyes went to each of the shops. Had she come to visit one of them? Walking slowly toward the first, he looked in the small window filled with bottles and oddities. Deciding it was in her best interest to investigate further, he entered. If Claire was in trouble or ill, then she needed help and he would offer his services; however he wanted to know what he was dealing with first.

An elderly woman appeared, dressed in so many colors that Simon blinked several times just to assure himself his eyes had seen her accurately. He was fairly certain she was wearing every color of the rainbow, starting with the large yellow bow placed on the top of her tight grey curls.

"Good day to you. My name is Lord Kelkirk, and I would like to enquire after a lady who may have entered your establishment just minutes ago. She was dressed entirely in black." The woman didn't offer a nod or smile of encouragement, just studied him with her faded eyes. The scent of dried herbs was almost overpowering, and he could feel a sneeze coming as he took a few moments to look around him. Hanging from every available space was an array of dried things. Some were herbs and others appeared to be the appendages of dead animals. All were covered in dust.

"No lady of that description has entered this shop, sir."

"You're sure," Simon questioned. After all, she was elderly and may just need another prod. His uncle was getting on in years and could be vague upon occasion.

"Because a body is old it does not mean it's dimwitted, sir. If I says no woman of that description has entered this shop today, then she ain't."

"Would you tell me if she had?" Simon questioned. The woman cackled just as Simon thought a witch would. Pinching the bridge of his nose, he attempted to hold back a sneeze. Once started, he was unsure he could stop without leaving the shop.

"Well now, that depends on what a person is willing to pay for the information."

Snorting, Simon handed over several coins, which she promptly tucked into her bodice.

"No woman of that description has come to this shop today," she said with a wide, toothless smile that left Simon with no doubts he had just been hoodwinked.

"Very cunning, madam."

"You needs to rise a bit earlier to get anything over Bea Bugs, my lord."

Simon's eyes narrowed. "Is that really your name?"

"Course not. Don't know as my ma had many brains, yet don't think she'd come up with something like that. Has quite a ring to it, don't it?"

"An illustrious title, Miss Bugs, for a colorful lady." Giving her a bow because really, she had bettered him without blinking and he, gullible fool he was for thinking that with age came a dulling of wits, had allowed it to happen. Pushing aside what looked to be a hanging bunch of small, pointed teeth, he then left.

Shaking his head a short while later, he walked from the last shop with as much information as he'd had when he'd entered the first and considerably lighter pockets. No one had known anything about a lady dressed in black. So if she had not come here to visit a shop, then perhaps she, like he, had been passing through the lane en route to meeting someone. But why would the proper Miss Belmont have cause to meet anyone here? It made no sense at all.

Now hopelessly late to meet Daniel and purchase the horse, Simon made his way back to the main street and then toward the club. He wouldn't mention this little incident to his friend, not until he knew what the hell had just happened. And he would find out. In fact, he would be questioning Claire when next he saw her, which would very possibly be this evening.

His first impulse had been to storm around to her house and demand an explanation, but that would achieve nothing. She would simply refuse to see him, and in turn, her family would be alerted to whatever she was doing. He was fairly certain her brother had no idea she was skulking about dressed like an old crone in a lane that, whilst not the worst in London, was hardly the best.

Was she meeting a lover? Simon had to stop while he thought that over. Claire Belmont with a lover. No, it did not settle well with him, nor did he want it to. Ignoring the sharp, stabbing pain in his chest, he started walking once more.

Was she ill? Had she come here to get something she desperately needed for her health? This thought made the pain intensify. Claire always looked a picture of good health, to his mind. Of course that was because she was always perfectly dressed, her hair never out of place. In fact Claire did everything perfectly, never did anything that would raise the collective eyes of society. She smiled when she should and spoke about the correct topics to the correct people. She was the epitome of all a young lady should be, at least until today. Today she'd behaved irrationally, and he was determined to find out why.

DEAR GOD, what had she just done? Claire Belmont fell back against the worn seats of the hackney. She had just hit Viscount Kelkirk in the face with her reticule, which held a heavy pouch of coins, and that was after fleeing from him like a crazed idiot.

"No, no, no." Claire felt the pressure of tears behind her eyes but would not give in to them. What should she do now? Pulling the note from her reticule, she reread the words.

Your brother left something behind in France, Miss Belmont, when his regiment passed through. If you want to know what, then meet me in Tuttle Lane at eleven o'clock tomorrow. Bring money and come alone.

Folding it once more, she tucked it back into her reticule. She dared not go back to the lane now because Lord Kelkirk could still be there and he would pounce on her, demanding answers to the questions that would be rolling around in his head. Besides, her family would notice her absence if she stayed away much longer. Claire could only hope that whomever had written that note made contact with her again, because she could not take the risk of returning to Tuttle Lane today.

Rushing off alone this morning had probably not been the action of a rational person, yet Anthony's death had nearly destroyed Claire, and if there was something of his left in the world, then she wanted it and did not want her elder brother to do anything to deter her from getting it. Yes, it could be a hoax, yet something inside Claire had believed it wasn't. When she'd read that note, something had gripped her—an urgency that had forced her to take a risk to see what Anthony had left behind in France. Now she would have to wait and hope that soon she would receive more correspondence.

How would she face Lord Kelkirk this evening? It was the Harrison ball and everyone would be there, so he definitely would be unless he fell ill—really ill—this afternoon. *That doesn't make me a bad person, wishing an illness on a man I don't wish to see.*

"Yes it does," she sighed. It made her a very bad person.

Perhaps she could fall suddenly ill? Tell her mother she had a sore head and needed quiet and bed rest? But then what about tomorrow evening and the one after that? She'd have to face him sometime, and knowing Simon as she did, she knew he would never let what happened today drop until he had all the facts. He was tenacious and would hunt her down until he had answers to all his questions. Simon did not understand social boundaries or the restrictions these placed on a person. If he wanted to ask a question, no matter how delicate, he did. She would need to stay composed in his company when next they met, because only he could provoke her enough to drop her calm façade and turn into a sharp-tongued shrew in seconds.

All she'd had to do today to quash his curiosity was say

something like, 'Lord Kelkirk, what a surprise to see you here. My maid comes here often and today I accompanied her to see what has her so excited.' She could have then offered a polite titter, perhaps, and asked after his health. Why hadn't she? If Claire was good at one thing, it was social chatter. She'd done nothing because she'd panicked. The fear of exposure had rendered her speechless, and she had reacted instinctively and without thought. No one had known she was going to Tuttle Lane, and she'd wanted it kept a secret, so she'd fled like a fool. Of course, now he did know she'd been there and with a few well-placed words, could make her life difficult.

Walking from the hackney minutes later toward her family's townhouse, Claire counted the six steps up as she trod them and then stepped over the small crack on the top one, as she did every time she left or entered the house. The door opened before she reached for it and her brother's butler, who used to be her father's butler, stood waiting for her.

"Hello, Plimley."

He looked at her intently for several seconds before he spoke. "Miss Belmont, are you well?"

"Yes, thank you, Plimley," Claire said, stepping inside.

Plimley had been Claire's friend when she did not have many. He had played cards with her, listened as she'd practiced piano and read her books when her brother or mother could not. He'd been a constant in her life and was someone she cared for very much.

"And how was your slumber last night, Miss Belmont?"

Lowering her eyes, Claire mumbled something vague and waved her hand about. Plimley knew her sleeping habits were not good, just like he always knew if something was worrying her. However, she was not about to get into that with him now.

"Are you wanting these taken to your room, Miss Belmont?" the butler added, looking at the faded cloak and bonnet he had just taken from her.

Claire was used to Plimley, having known him since she was ten, however sometimes he still made her blink. He was possibly one of the most handsome men she had ever seen. His hair was thick and blonde even at fifty-five years old; he had the bluest eyes and kindest smile of any person she knew. Her mother's friends—any woman callers, in fact—swooned over him. Even men stopped and stared at him, yet he remained calm and surprisingly un-conceited always. Even when Lady Carmichael had pretended to trip and fall into his arms, he'd simply righted her and remained unflustered as she'd twittered about his strong arms and firm, muscled torso.

"Yes, take them to my room, please," Claire said and she could hear the tremor in her voice. She was tired, having not slept last night with worry. She needed to reach her room and rest, and then she could think about what next she would do about that note.

"Is there a problem, Miss Belmont? Something I may help you with?"

"I'm well, thank you, Plimley," Claire said, patting his hand.

"Perhaps a nap before this evening's entertainment would set you to rights?"

Plimley was a watcher. He knew what each member of the Belmont family needed before he or she needed it, and most especially Claire. She'd been fooling herself when she'd thought to deter him from her tired state.

"Yes, you are right, Plimley, but I shall visit with mother and Mathew before I do so."

"I shall see to preparing a herbal tisane to calm your thoughts, Miss Belmont, and have it placed in your room."

Claire began to turn away and then faced the butler once more. She squeezed his hand briefly. "Plimley, I have no right to ask this of you, but if I ever marry, will you come with me to whatever household I end up in and be my butler?"

"I would be honored."

"And Amanda and Liam, of course," Claire added. Plimley was married to one of her brother's maids, a pretty, sweet-natured woman who had a practical soul and did not fall about the place swooning when her husband was near. It was the belief among the staff here that if the Plimley child Liam, aged eight, who was already showing signs of resembling his sire, turned out as handsome as either of his parents, then no woman within five miles of him would be safe.

"I shall be sure to tell her there will be a move in the future for us all."

Claire's smile wobbled slightly, and then she drew back her shoulders and made for the stairs. Gripping the banister, she walked up slowly, the carpet muffling the sounds of her footfalls. The Belmont townhouse was decorated tastefully, if a little fussily, thanks to her mother. If there was an available space, then Lady Belmont tended to place something into it. The staff grumbled incessantly about the dusting, and many things had been broken over the years, however her mother rarely noticed, or if she did, she simply went out and purchased something new. Nodding to the portrait of her father, Claire turned left at the top. She had not known the late Lord Belmont well, as he'd died when she was a child, yet her mother said the portrait depicted him perfectly, and if that was the case, she was sure he had been just a touch wicked. His smile held a knowing gleam that always made her own lips tilt.

She could hear the sound of someone tapping a spoon against his or her cup as she reached the door to the morning room, where she knew her family would be. Pushing aside thoughts of Anthony and the note, she walked through with a forced smile on her face. She'd noted that if her smile was wide enough, no one noticed if she was troubled. Most people were busy worrying about their own problems. Claire entered quietly to the sounds of her mother gossiping about the flirtatious behavior of Miss Tattingham last night.

"Atrocious. I hardly knew where to look when she lifted her skirts to show Lord Milton her ankles."

"I'm sure it was an accident, mother. Miss Tattingham has been nothing but polite in my company."

"Of course she is polite to you, Mathew—she wants to marry you. Or anyone with a fortune," Lady Belmont added.

"So the only reason I'm worthy of her attention is because I'm eligible, mother? I can't tell you how happy that thought makes me."

Lady Belmont sniffed, which was meant to mean something, however Claire was not sure what.

"Claire, where have you been?" Her brother noted her then and rose as she moved into the room. Tall and lean, Lord Mathew Belmont was the image of their late father, with his thick straight brown hair and green eyes. However he did not have the twinkle, nor was he even the tiniest bit wicked. In fact, he was serious-minded and humorless. Older than Claire by six years, he had been the one to censure her when required and had been more father than brother to her for as long as she could remember.

"I went to visit with a friend," Claire said calmly.

"Alone?" He lifted one eyebrow to glare down at her. She always found that action irritating, even more so when she was tired. In fact, everything compounded when she was tired. People tended to annoy her more, noises seemed louder, and small things like a hole in the end of her gloves could make her angry or weepy.

"I took a maid," she lied and then smiled sweetly.

"No you didn't."

"How do you know I didn't?" Claire felt the smile slip and struggled to hold it in place.

"I asked."

"For pity's sake, Mathew, I'm twenty years old—practically a spinster. I do not need a maid to visit a friend. Nor do I need you checking on my movements with the household staff."

His brows now met in the middle. "I will check on your movements until you are married. And what friend did you visit at such an early hour?"

"My favorite one," Claire snapped, stepping around him, thus, to her mind, ending the conversation. "Mother, I'm a bit weary today, so I thought to have a nap before this evening. Will you please excuse me from any activities you may have planned?"

Where Mathew looked like their father, Claire and Anthony had taken after their mother. Her strawberry blonde curls had now turned grey, and her hazel eyes were shadowed with the grief she still carried from losing her husband and youngest son. Yet Lady Eliza Belmont was as lively as she had always been.

"Of course, darling. You must look your best this evening. I have great hopes for you this season, especially as we now have a wonderful crop of noblemen in town."

"I have just been likened to a field of wheat," Her brother said.

Claire felt the silly urge to giggle at his disgusted expression, so she pressed a hand to her mouth to keep herself from talking further. She was tired enough that it would not take much to set her off, and she had no intentions of falling into a fit of hysteria in front of Mathew.

"Well, she has already turned down three proposals, so let

us hope for someone to fill her exacting standards this season."

"Would you have me wed to a man I did not respect, Mathew?

"No, Claire, that was never my wish for you." Mathew said solemnly.

"I'm sure I will find the perfect man soon and you shall be rid of me," Claire added and then forced out a laugh so her family knew she was merely making light of the matter, when in fact the topic was a painful one for her. She had nearly reached the door before Mathew's voice stopped her.

"Are you well, Claire?

"Of course I'm well, Mathew. Why would you think otherwise?" Claire kept her tone light as she reached out to grab the door handle to steady herself. He saw too much and she did not want him to know about the note, so she kept her eyes on the panel of wood before her.

"It is not like you to take to your bed in the middle of the day, sister."

"I have a slight headache, Mathew, nothing further. A short nap will put me to rights."

Before he could say anything further, she left the parlor, closing the door softly behind her.

Her room overlooked the gardens, but as the curtains were drawn when she entered, she saw only the muted shadows of furniture. Shutting the door behind her, Claire felt the pain in her head start to ease. It had begun to throb after her encounter with Lord Kelkirk. Lord, how was she to face him tonight? *Not now, Claire.* Right now, she needed to rest, as she would need all her wits about her when next they met. Her maid arrived and she was soon down to her chemise. Picking up the glass holding the tisane that Plimley had prepared, off the bedside table, she swallowed the vile liquid with a shudder and then slid between the sheets.

What had Anthony left behind in France? Would she receive another note soon? How was she to avoid Lord Kelkirk? Staring into the darkness, Claire let the thoughts tumble around inside her head until finally she felt the bliss of sleep settle over her. With another tired sigh, she turned on her side and was soon slumbering.

…

When the Belmont's arrived at the Harrison ball, the rooms were already filled with guests. Smothering a yawn, Claire tried to shake the fog from her head. The sleeping tisane had given her sleep but also horrid, heated dreams in which she was clad in only her undergarments and Lord Kelkirk stood there laughing at her. She was feeling listless and dull-witted, which was never a good sign when she was stepping into the bosom of some of the ton's more voracious gossips.

"Come along, Claire. You're wool-gathering." Mathew held out his arm, and she gladly took it, feeling better now she was anchored to something solid.

The season was well advanced, and of course Lady Harrison had invited everyone and everyone had accepted, as there had been whispers that the king himself would arrive. Claire knew this was a ploy quite a few of the hostesses used to ensure their gatherings were successful.

"Quite a crush," Lady Belmont said, smiling. Claire's mother, unlike Claire, loved a crush.

"God help us all."

"I thought you enjoyed these things, Mathew." Claire looked up at her brother as he spoke. He was handsome in his black jacket and grey and burgundy striped waistcoat.

"Being jostled, spilling beverages on myself as people pass, dancing with silly, empty-headed debutants. Of course I love it, sister."

Claire looked forward as they walked deeper into the

room and then back at her brother. "If that is indeed the case, Mathew, then you hide it very well." Obviously, she was not the only Belmont sibling with acting talent.

"Would you have me walk about scowling, Claire?"

"Do you want to scowl?"

He looked down at her briefly. "Constantly."

"I'm sorry. I thought I was the only one who was not overly enamored with these events, brother."

They stopped behind several other people, and once again Mathew looked down at her, his eyes searching her face. "Perhaps if you had asked, I would have told you."

Claire didn't know what to say to that because she'd never shared confidences or secrets with Mathew. It had been Anthony she was close to, not her older brother.

"Excuse me, children. I see a friend I would like to talk with. I shall find you both later in the evening."

The Belmont siblings watched their mother move with ease through the crowd and disappear.

"One wonders how she saw her friend when I can only just see over the heads closest to me," Mathew said.

"She has been to more of these events than both of us put together, Mathew, but she never seems to tire of them. Do you think it is something lacking in her or us that we cannot find the same enjoyment?'

Mathew didn't answer her immediately, as he navigated them around a large, chatting group of guests, but Claire could see he was thinking carefully about what to say next.

"I would never suggest mother's intelligence is beneath ours, Claire. However I will say she finds joy in her surroundings far more easily than you or I."

"Acceptance, Mathew. She is far more accepting than us, surely?"

He let out a little snuffle that was his way of showing humor. Mathew rarely laughed out loud. Indeed, perhaps he was more like her than Claire had realized. He rarely expressed emotions. "We should probably host a ball one day. Mother is constantly harping on about it."

God, just the thought made her shudder. All those preparations and invitations. The planning would take weeks. "Must we?"

"But how are we to secure you a husband if your hostessing prowess is not displayed to the eligible bachelors, sister?"

Claire looked up at her brother with narrowed eyes. He looked calmly back.

"You had better be teasing me, brother. For in truth, were you not, I may be forced to seek retribution." She was surprised to realize they were actually having a conversation that she was enjoying. Usually Mathew was lecturing her, and she was snapping back at him. They had not laughed in each other's company for a long time, especially since their brother's death.

He snuffled again and continued walking. "What will it be, Claire? Frogs or insects in my bed?"

This time she laughed, remembering their childhood antics "Frogs, I think."

"You are about to be claimed for your first dance, sister, and for the record, I would never accept Lord Smythe's suite, were he to offer for you."

Claire eyed the tall man heading her way. "Why?"

"My horse could outthink him."

"Mathew!" Claire gasped, giggling behind her hand.

"Good evening, Lord Belmont, Miss Belmont."

"How does Arthur fare today, Smythe? I heard he was not in good form."

Who was Arthur? Claire thought, looking from her brother to Lord Smythe.

"Much better, Belmont. He ate a full meal before I left for

the ball, and I have hopes of letting him outside again in the morning."

"Who is Arthur?" Claire questioned.

Mathew turned to face her, his eyes twinkling—a rare sight. "Lord Smythe's piglet. He takes it everywhere with him. It even lives in the house."

"In my room," Lord Smythe said, nodding his head several times.

"Well then," Claire said because she could think of nothing further to add to this silly conversation.

"Perhaps you will take your brother's word more seriously in future," Mathew said in her ear. Then he kissed her cheek.

"May I have this dance, Miss Belmont?"

"Thank you, Lord Smythe, I would be honored." Claire gave her brother a bright, very false smile and then let Lord Smythe lead her onto the dance floor.

CHAPTER TWO

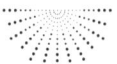

*C*laire tried to focus on her partners as she danced the next set, yet she found herself constantly surveying the crowd, searching for Simon. She was determined to avoid him for as long as possible.

"Can I get you some refreshment, Miss Belmont?"

"No thank you, Lord Cavell, I shall be fine."

After he had excused himself, Claire stood on her toes and looked around the room. She couldn't see the black and silver hair of Lord Kelkirk, however that did not mean he was not here. She would keep moving, circling the room, and then if she saw him, she could nip behind the nearest statue.

"Hello, Claire."

"Eva, how wonderful to see you—it seems such an age," Claire declared as her friend appeared before her.

"I saw you Tuesday, Claire—surely not an age, as this is only Thursday."

"Perhaps not an age then," she added, looking over her friend's shoulder. Was that Lord Kelkirk? He was tall and that man was tall. Although from this distance she could not determine if he had the distinctive black and silver hair.

"Who are you looking for, Claire?"

"Looking for?" Claire brought her eyes back to her friend.

The Duchess of Stratton was giving her a puzzled look. Her head tilted slightly to one side while she studied Claire through pretty, sapphire blue eyes. "You appear to be searching for someone."

"No, just being nosey."

"Well, it is hard not to be at occasions such as these. This is my second season, and I am still constantly surprised by the clothing and antics of the guests. Have you seen Lord and Lady Pepper?" Eva asked.

"Oh lord, what are they wearing tonight?" Eva made a great show of looking about her.

"Matching lemon, and whilst you may not think lemon a disturbing color, this is."

"Disturbing how?"

"It's the brightest lemon and quite hurts the eye, and her dress is fashioned like his jacket, with little buttons running up the front and a panel of piping down the skirt to make it look as though she has trousers on."

She just had to see that, Claire thought climbing to her toes, which gained her nothing, as most of the men were taller than her, and some of the ladies. "Who do you believe dresses them? I'm thinking it's someone they've done something grievous to. Someone who has revenge on her mind and is slowly extracting it, outfit by outfit."

Eva laughed, which made her look lovelier, if that was possible. The duchess was a beautiful woman, and had Claire not been her friend, she would have disliked her intensely. She had thick, raven locks and the kind of figure that made men sigh. She looked stunning in whatever she chose to wear, which tonight was an emerald green creation that made her look like a goddess.

"How is it possible you look like that after the birth of

your child only a few months ago? I saw how big your stomach was, after all. Tis most unfair, and may I add, were I not your friend, I would be quite put out that if anything, you appear lovelier."

Waving the compliment aside, Eva continued with their conversation. That was another thing about her that Claire liked—she was totally unaware of her beauty. "It would not be quite so bad if Lady Pepper was not so…"

"Fleshy, elephantine, paunchy? Come, Eva, I'm sure you can come up with a descriptive word."

Eva pinched her friend's arm.

"Ouch! I was only stating the truth. We all know Lady Pepper has eaten one éclair too many." Claire climbed to her toes once more and surveyed the room. Eva thought she was seeking the Peppers, however she was looking for Lord Kelkirk.

"I'm sure you're looking for someone and not telling me who."

Eva may appear sweet and innocent, but she was also intelligent and tenacious when required.

"I'm searching for the Peppers, as you very well know, Duchess. Now tell me, how is my darling Georgia?"

The puzzled look left her friend's eyes as her lips tilted into a smile. The one a woman got when she fell in love or had a child. It never failed to signal a kind of longing in Claire, to experience such total and utter devotion to another person.

"Oh, Claire, she is so sweet. Why, just yesterday, she rolled over twice. We shall not be staying long this evening, as both Daniel and I are loath to leave her over long."

Happy to let her friend talk about the baby while she kept an eye on the people around them, Claire listened with one ear.

"I am bringing her to visit with you and your mother

tomorrow. I saw Lady Belmont briefly a few minutes ago, and she told me I was to come."

"That's Mother for you. She demands and everyone falls in with her wishes. However in this case they coincide with mine nicely. I found the sweetest little doll—"

"Claire, you gave her a gift last week. You shouldn't spoil her so much. Simon is the same. He's always popping in with something tucked under his arm."

"Is he?" Even the mention of his name made Claire's heart thump. Could she avoid him for the remainder of the season?

"He carries her around in his arms the entire time he's visiting. Daniel says it's the most emotion he's ever seen him show a woman besides his aunt."

"Aunt?" Claire couldn't remember meeting his aunt.

"His aunt and uncle live at his estate, I believe, and he is very close to them."

"Good evening, Claire."

"Good evening, Daniel." Claire smiled as the Duke of Stratton approached. He instantly slipped an arm around his wife's waist. Their marriage had had a tumultuous beginning, yet it had grown into something that was the envy of many, and the birth of their daughter had only strengthened those bonds.

"We were just discussing Simon's devotion to our daughter, darling."

"Yes. It's an amazing thing, really, considering he usually has no time for anyone but himself."

Claire and Anthony had grown up with Daniel, and for many years they had been close, until the death of her brother when, distraught, she had turned her back on everyone. It had taken Eva stepping into both their lives to bridge the gap between them.

"As he's your dearest friend, your grace, one wonders how you speak of your enemies," she said, enjoying teasing the man who had once accompanied her over the hills of her home for hours, whilst they endeavored to find a tree tall enough to climb so they could see London.

Daniel Stratton was a big, handsome man. He was far more serious than his friend Lord Kelkirk, but had been highly regarded as quite the marital catch for young woman, before he wed Eva.

"It never pays to let Simon know you care for him or he takes advantage of you, Claire," the duke said. "And now, if you will excuse us, I am going to dance with my wife."

"Of course."

Claire watched Daniel lift Eva's hand to his lips before placing it on his arm. Eva's smile was soft as she looked up at her husband, and Claire could almost feel the love that flowed between them. She wanted that—a love so strong that you felt what the other half of you felt. Pain, happiness—your life was so entwined in another's that to be parted was almost too much to bear. She noted the look they shared, then a secret smile as he swung her into his arms. Sighing, Claire turned away. They had ruined her with their love. Now she refused to settle for anything less.

Looking up, she saw him then—Lord Kelkirk—making his way through the horde of guests, stopping occasionally when someone talked to him. She supposed he was a good-looking man. It was the hair, of course—the black threaded with silver. It made him stand out from the men around him. The fact that he was tall and clothes seemed to sit on him effortlessly, and he carried himself with a natural elegance that made a person look—especially if that person was a woman. Not her, of course. Claire and Simon had drawn swords long ago and merely tolerated each other for the sake of their friends. However she was a woman, so she occasionally did look.

He wore charcoal this evening. His jacket fit him to

perfection. His waistcoat was silver and blue, and with his white shirt and neck cloth, she supposed he was one of the more stylish men in attendance. As if he knew she was studying him, his eyes swung to where she stood. Claire could feel the intensity of that grey gaze even if she could not see it from here. Desperate to escape before he reached her, she sought someone to save her from the upcoming confrontation. She would need all her wits about her when that moment came, and tonight was not that night.

"Mr. Rynell, I believe this is your dance?" Claire said, placing her hand on the sleeve of the man who was standing with a group of men to her right. He stared at her open-mouthed.

"I…is it? Of course it is." He recovered quickly; she had to give him that. Offering her a strained smile, he then led her onto the dance floor.

"Miss Belmont, if I may have a word—"

"Not now, Lord Kelkirk. As you can see, I am to dance with Mr. Rynell." Widening her smile as much as she could without causing herself pain, Claire sailed past Simon as he scowled at her, his grey eyes narrowing as she proceeded to chatter like a debutante to her bemused dance partner.

She danced and danced and danced. Never taking a break, Claire simply went from one partner to another until she feared her feet had blisters. Every time she thought to stop, she would see him, Lord Kelkirk, leaning on a wall, watching her intently. She even danced with Lord Pepper, who was preening over the interest his jacket was causing. The color was so bright that looking at it made her head start to ache.

"You must tell me the name of your wife's tailor, my lord," Claire said, simply because she wanted to make sure to avoid her at all costs.

"I fear she is ours exclusively, my dear, and my darling

wife would be distressed, were I to give the name of the establishment to anyone."

Claire managed to say something complimentary and tried to keep her distance from Simon, who had decided to stop staring at her long enough to partner Miss Hadfield in this dance. When it finally ended she was sure she could not dance another step, so she accompanied Lord Pepper to where a group of acquaintances stood, and once he left, she shuffled sideways to hide behind them. Peeking over the shoulder of one of the women, she looked for Simon but could not see him. Seizing the chance to escape, she made her way toward the back of the room. Dropping her head, she bent at the knees and moved through the throng, hoping no one noticed what she was doing.

"Are you well, Miss Belmont?"

"Yes thank you, Mr. Tattler. I am looking for my mother."

The man looked at her bent legs but said nothing further, so Claire moved on. It was not the easiest position to walk in —in fact, her thighs were starting to cramp, especially after the exercise she had just undertaken—yet she had no intention of straightening until she found a place to hide.

Reaching the wall, Claire straightened but kept her shoulders hunched and head lowered as she moved along it. Arriving at the opening, she hurried through, and down a hall to the door at the end. With a deep sigh of relief, Claire straightened to her full height as she stepped into the cool night air.

"HELLO, Claire. How are you this evening?" Simon said, walking through the door and moving to where she now stood in the shadows. He heard her indrawn breath, and watched as she took a step backward, and then another until she was pressed against the stone balustrade. Simon closed the distance between them, stopping directly in front of her.

He had returned Miss Hadfield to her mother after their dance, and then looked for Claire. He'd found her slipping through a door, and followed. She'd hoped to avoid him, but he had no intention of allowing that to happen. He had questions he wanted answered.

"Lord Kerkirk, how lovely to see you. I hope you are enjoying the evening?"

He was impressed. She didn't stutter, although the moonlight allowed him to see how wide her eyes were, and he could hear the rasp of her breathing. "Very much, Claire, and you? How are you feeling this evening?"

Her eyes widened briefly. "Very well, thank you, my lord."

"I had not realized you had such a love of dancing."

"Yes, I enjoy it very much, my lord."

"You've definitely hidden it well then, as before tonight I have never seen you partner so many men--one after the other without pausing for breath. Quite a testament to your stamina."

She wanted to say something cutting but instead pressed her lips together firmly, forming a straight crease that almost folded in on itself.

"And it appears you have suffered no ill effects from looking at Lord Pepper's waistcoat over long."

She clamped her lips together harder.

"Excellent. Now that we have established your love of dancing and observed the correct greeting, perhaps you can tell me why you were in that lane today dressed like a servant? And why you ran into me—"

"You ran into me!"

He knew she wished to retract those words as soon as she had spoken them. But it had always been that way with them; he could provoke her into retaliation and make her lose her composure with only a few well-placed words. "Why were you in that lane alone today, Claire?"

"I have no wish to answer that or any of your questions, Lord Kelkirk."

Simon had often wondered why she intrigued him. Most evenings he found himself searching for her in a crowded room, his eyes drawn to the sweet bow that formed her lips into a pout. Her brows were delicately arched and she usually had one elevated in a haughty manner when he was near. Simon had always thought Claire Belmont alluring. However with him she was rarely sweet; in fact, he would say she was prickly and cutting and never missed an opportunity to take him to task. She wasn't comfortable with him and he'd never been sure why.

"I have a bruise on my chin, Claire. I think I deserve some kind of answer."

"For that I am sorry," she said slowly, her eyes looking at the dark mark on his jaw. "It was never my intention to hurt you."

"Why were you in that lane today, Claire?" Simon stepped closer, forcing her eyes up to meet his.

"I will not be intimidated by you, Lord Kelkirk, therefore please step back."

She sounded calm, yet Simon saw the wariness in her eyes.

"Whatever the reason, it was important enough that you had no one accompanying you and had disguised yourself in old clothes. Were you collecting something or meeting someone?"

"What I do is of no concern to you, my lord, nor do I care for your line of questioning."

She was trying to remain in control, but Simon knew her well enough to see she was scared and he didn't like that, because he'd never seen fear in her eyes before. But most of all, he didn't like to think she was ill or suffering in any way. He had thought long and hard about what might have put her in that lane today and none of his ideas had been good ones. "Are you sick, Claire?"

"Please, Simon, just leave this alone."

The use of his name surprised him. She was never informal with him or anyone besides Daniel and Eva. Claire kept people at a distance and behaved at all times as a lady of her birth and rank should. She was the woman most mothers held up to their daughters as the pinnacle of excellence. *Miss Belmont has such impeccable manners,* Simon had heard parent's say to their offspring. *You should try to emulate her.*

"I could help you if you would just tell me what's wrong, Claire." She looked away, but he was not having that. He touched her chin, lifting it until their eyes met. He saw the pallor of her skin in the moonlight. There were dark smudges beneath her eyes that no amount of powder could hide. He cupped her cheek, running his thumb down the satin skin, enjoying the warmth of her. "Talk to me, Claire."

To his surprise, she briefly leaned in to him, closing her eyes on a gentle sigh.

"You look tired."

She wrapped her fingers around his wrist "Please, Simon, do not pursue this matter, I beg of you."

"Claire, please tell me why you were in that lane."

"There is nothing to tell. I was with my maid shopping, and you startled me."

"I saw no maid." Simon knew the moment of weakness had gone when she pushed his hand aside.

"She was in a shop, and I would be grateful if you did not continue with this line of questioning now or in the future."

Without physically restraining her, Simon could not stop her from stepping around him, so instead, he watched her walk away and disappear back through the doors. Following a few minutes later, he saw her beside Daniel and Eva.

"Hello, Simon."

"Daniel," Simon said, stopping beside Claire, standing as close as propriety allowed and close enough to unnerve her.

"Good evening, Duchess." He bowed deeply. "May I say how beautiful you are in that dress? The color is really quite something on you."

"She may believe your compliments were they not delivered with such a ferocious frown on your face, Kelkirk."

Simon glared at his friend, who simply smiled back.

"I was not scowling—I was squinting," Simon said, wondering what had come over him. He didn't squint. Actually, he rarely scowled either. It was Claire. She was addling his wits.

"Ah, I believe for some, loss of sight comes with age."

"You're older than me," Simon snapped.

"And surprisingly I have perfect eyesight. Perhaps I'm just aging better than you."

They were longstanding friends, he and the Duke of Stratton, and for many years they had lived the bachelor life with ease. However Daniel had married Eva, and after a tumultuous beginning, they had grown to love each other very much. Watching his friend look at his wife now, his eyes full of love and devotion, Simon felt an arrow of jealousy. He'd never wanted wedded bliss, or even the companionship of marriage, yet seeing the love Daniel and Eva shared, he wondered if he'd been wrong.

"Is that a paunch?" Simon felt marginally better when the duke looked down at his stomach. Of course it was flat, yet the taunt had produced a reaction, as he'd wanted.

"And they say women are vain."

Claire's words gave Simon the opportunity to look at her, and he noted she had recovered fully from the momentary weakness she had shown him just minutes ago. In fact, she had that complacent smile firmly in place and was once again the impeccable Miss Belmont. He wanted to shake her.

"Are you suggesting I'm vain, Miss Belmont?"

"Of course I am. In fact, I would go so far as saying you spend as much time on your appearance as I."

"Daniel's the same, Claire—he spends a ridiculous amount of time in front of the mirror tying and retying his neck cloth," Eva said.

"No I don't," the duke said, looking put out. "You spend an age choosing jewelry. In fact I don't start my dressing until you've reached that stage because I know it gives me a good thirty minutes to ready myself."

"That is not true," the duchess protested.

"Yes it is, and before this escalates, we're dancing," Daniel said, taking his wife's hand and towing her onto the dance floor, leaving Claire and Simon alone once more.

"Do you have digestion trouble, Claire?" Simon questioned as he watched Daniel place Eva in the line across from him. "Or a delicate illness that would account for your secrecy?"

"I beg your pardon? How dare you ask me such a personal question in company."

"I shall call upon you tomorrow then, and ask when we are not in company."

She didn't show any outward signs of anger, but the glare she turned on him would have felled the average man.

"I have no wish for you to call upon me, my lord. Ever," she added.

Had anyone passed at the moment, they would have thought the very respectable Miss Belmont was merely conversing with him; she hadn't raised her voice above what was expected in such a gathering.

"In fact I would be quite happy if we never spoke again."

"You wound me, Miss Belmont, and there was me thinking we were friends," Simon drawled when he wanted to roar at her—wrap his hands around the tops of her slender arms and shake the answer from her. "And just so we're clear on the matter of you in that lane today. I will keep asking about it until you tell me why you were so upset, and more importantly, why you were there alone."

"Why do you care?"

Simon shouldn't have been happy to see her composure slip slightly as she whispered the words at him, but he was.

"Because I think something is very wrong to have sent you there today, and I want to help."

Panic clenched her fists, and then she exhaled, and regained control.

"Very well. If you insist on knowing, then I must tell you. However I had given her my word."

"Her?" Simon questioned, watching Claire closely.

"One of my maids suffers from terrible headaches, and she was bedridden today, so I offered to get her a tonic."

Simon did not speak straightaway, instead letting the silence draw out between them. Usually he was very good at silence; even in a room filled with noise, he had a knack of using it to get people talking. However Claire was more than equal to the task. In fact, she smiled at someone passing and waved her hand before looking back at him.

"You must be very close with her to have gone to such lengths, Claire. Disguising yourself in those old, dark clothes and wandering about in that shady lane with no one to protect you. Such dedication to your staff is to be commended." She didn't speak, so he continued. "But if that is indeed the truth, I wonder why you felt the need to run when you knew it was me that you had collided with."

"I have no further wish to discuss the matter, and will thank you to let it rest now."

One thing Simon knew about Claire Belmont was that she was scrupulously honest. In fact he'd never known her to lie, until tonight.

"You're lying to me, Claire, and that only concerns me more." Simon's words were softly spoken but he knew she heard them.

She didn't speak again. Instead she walked away. Head high, she made her way slowly through the crowd until he could no longer see her. Only then did Simon release the breath he had not known he was holding.

CHAPTER THREE

Simon rose early the morning after the Harrison ball. Pulling on his dressing gown, he then made his way through the house and out into the gardens. The air was crisp as the new day began to dawn, and the smell of fires being stoked around him started to chase away the more earthy scents of his garden. He loved being outside; this was where he felt happiest, and if his fingers were immersed in soil, then he was even happier. Raised by his aunt and uncle, both of whom loved the outdoors and puttered in their glasshouses constantly, he had developed that love too. Simon knew about plants and herbs; he understood what grew best in the shade and what flourished in the sun. Aunt Penelope and Uncle Peter had taught him endlessly about such things, and he'd soaked up every word. Watching a plant grow that he had nurtured from a seedling was a special gift and one he appreciated more and more as he grew older.

His staff were used to him now, and rarely threw him a sideways glance as he wandered barefoot up and down the rows of plants and trees he tended. He crushed a few precious leaves in his hand and smelt the freshness that reminded him of Luxley, his estate. Dropping to his knees beside a bed of violets, he pulled a few weeds. These were his aunt's favorites, so he had planted them for the rare occasions she visited London. This relaxed him, gave him clarity, and this was where he came when he needed to think.

Was she sick? Was Claire Belmont so sick that she had to sneak out of her house alone to get whatever it was she needed? Diseases like consumption, the slow wasting of the body that made it grow weak and fatigued, filtered through his head. She didn't look sick; in fact, she'd looked as beautiful to his eyes as she always did. The only other option was that she had arranged to meet someone in that lane, but whom? Last night as he'd laid for hours staring into the darkness, Simon wondered if she was being blackmailed, yet he could not imagine what information anyone would have on her, as her reputation was pristine. Why couldn't he just leave it alone, let her have her secrets and walk away?

Pulling a weed with more force than required, Simon knew the answer to that question. The thought of her ill or in distress had settled uncomfortably in the pit of his stomach and it would not be dislodged until he had answers. He hated to admit it even to a bed of violets, but he cared about Claire Belmont's welfare far more than he should.

Rising, he wandered into his glasshouse to check on his seedlings and then made his way back inside. He would visit with Daniel and Eva—and his favorite small person, of course—this morning. Perhaps he could make a few subtle enquiries of Eva; she may know why Claire had been in that lane. He didn't want to alert Eva to his concerns, but maybe she would let something slip if he brought up Claire's name.

His bath was ready when he returned to his room, and, sinking into it, he watched his valet tsk at the dirt on the hem of his dressing gown and then tsk even louder at the dirty feet Simon draped over the edge of the tub.

"Slippers, my lord. Easy to put on and would save scrubbing several layers off your skin whenever you return from your gardens."

Simon had inherited Sullivan on a hunting trip to Ireland five years ago. He was flamboyant and opinionated and felt Simon would look like a chimney sweep in days if he was not with him at all times.

"I like the dirt under my toes," Simon said, knowing how much this annoyed Sullivan, as they'd had this conversation more times than he cared to count.

His valet snapped his mouth together and said nothing further, just scurried around the room selecting items of clothing for him to wear.

"For pity's sake, Sully, I am visiting friends. There is little need of such an extravagant waistcoat, surely?" Simon raised an eyebrow at the emerald and blue satin garment the man held reverently.

"You are to visit with the Duke and Duchess of Stratton, my lord. Such company deserves the very best attire."

"Bilby told me you threatened to tie Merlin down and scrub his neck and neck cloth if he did not wash both."

"Your butler is a man of impeccable cleanliness. However your head coachman is not, my lord."

Simon tried to remember the state of his head coachman's neck but couldn't.

"One of the parlor maids told me she was quite taken with Merlin, my lord, yet could not countenance his grubbiness."

"Therefore you have taken it upon yourself to help the budding romance along by suggesting he smells no better than a rodent?" Simon rose and dried himself.

"One tries, my lord," his valet said, handing Simon his

breeches. "I have also generously offered to assist him so he dresses in a manner that would ensure the maids did not run in the other direction, holding their noses. However as yet, he has not taken me up on this offer."

"I must tell him to run for the hills and not look back, then," Simon muttered. Rather than be insulted, Sullivan merely held out Simon's dark green jacket for him to slip into. He then took a small brush and began to apply it vigorously, which, of course, was not necessary, as the jacket had already been brushed repeatedly.

"Have mercy, Sully, I yield," Simon said tersely minutes later when he had been brushed until he gleamed.

"As you wish, my lord."

"Stop the wounded look. It doesn't wear with me, and for pity's sake, ensure my evening clothes are ready. Last night there was a crease in my waistcoat," Simon lied as he sailed from the room smiling. Sullivan would now spend the next hour examining said waistcoat.

"Coffee this morning please, Bilby." Settling in his chair, he picked up the paper his butler had laid out for him and opened the first page. He had managed to read most of it before Bilby returned with his drink.

"If I may discuss a matter with you, my lord."

Lowering the paper, Simon looked at his butler. "And the matter is?" he said politely. After all, his household was run by this man and it was run extremely well, to Simon's mind. If his butler had a problem, then it needed to be addressed at once.

"One of the housemaid's is with child, my lord, and Mrs. Beverly wishes to let her go, however I thought to speak with you first."

Had he a wife, this would be dealt with by her, Simon thought, resisting the urge to pinch the bridge of his nose.

"Do we know who the father is?

"Merlin, my lord,"

Well, it seemed a grubby collar and neck did not bother Simon's maid.

"And how old is the maid?"

"Eighteen, my lord."

"Her name is?"

"Jilly, my lord."

"Thank you for coming to me with this information, and you were right to do so, Bilby. Can you tell me what the housekeeper has to say on the matter?"

Bilby's expression became pinched as he mentioned Mrs. Dodd. "She's of the same opinion as Mrs. Beverly, the cook, my lord."

"And yet they are happy for Merlin to stay in my employ, which seems unjust, don't you think, Bilby?" Simon knew his views did not often coincide with the more bigoted members of society, yet he had not thought his staff so cutthroat in theirs.

"Indeed it does, my lord, and I fear that even if you keep her, they will not be fair to the girl."

Simon studied his immaculate butler. His age must be nearing sixty, he had a ring of silver hair around the back of his head but nothing on the top, and he was not what a person would call handsome, however he was comfortable to look at in a grandfatherly kind of way.

"And why do you not want to throw her from the house, Bilby, as my cook and housekeeper do?"

The man stood straighter, and the hands he had at his sides clenched briefly.

"Everyone makes mistakes, my lord, but it is not everyone who can come about because of them."

Simon wondered what mistake his butler had made. Perhaps one day he would ask, but for now he would deal with Jilly and Merlin.

"Wise words from a wise man, Bilby. Now if you will please bring Merlin to me at once, and after that, I will decide what needs to be done."

As soon as the butler left, Simon ate his breakfast slowly and then drank half the cup of coffee.

"You wish to see me, my lord?"

Simon questioned the eyesight of the maid who had declared Merlin handsome. His nose was crooked and he wore a permanent scowl. He had a head of brown hair that he was certain no amount of brushing would subdue, and on closer inspection, he did have a grubby air about him. His body was fit, which he supposed could be a lure for women, especially maids it seemed, and he was unequalled in handling horses and for that matter, carriages.

"I understand you have Jilly with child?"

The man raised his chin and nodded.

"And what did you plan to do about it?" Simon kept his eyes on Merlin. To his credit, he did not shuffle his feet or look away; in fact, he simply stared back.

"I love Jilly, my lord."

Merlin had been his head coachman for many years, however they rarely conversed. In fact, when they did, the barest minimum of words passed between them, usually to the purpose of making travel arrangements. In all honesty and to his shame, Simon could say he knew next to nothing about the man before him.

"Do you wish to marry her?"

"I do."

"Mrs. Beverly and Mrs. Dodd wish to let Jilly go, Merlin. Will there be a problem in my household if she stays after you wed?"

Rage flashed across the man's face briefly. "Mrs. Beverly and Mrs. Dodd think Jilly is a light skirt, if you'll beg my pardon for saying such a thing, my lord, however she is not. My Jilly is a fine woman."

Good god, the man was in love. He'd just strung an entire and passionate sentence together.

"Bilby!" Simon roared through the door, knowing his butler would be nearby.

"My lord?"

"Have Jilly brought up here at once."

"Yes, my lord."

"Where will you live, Merlin?" Simon said when the door had shut once more.

The chin rose again and this time Simon saw pride in the man's face.

"I'll provide for us."

"I'm sure you will, but I would like to help you with those provisions. If you find a house and need assistance securing it please let me know. I will then organize it on your behalf and we shall work through a suitable payment scheme for you both."

"I'll provide for us," he said again, thrusting out his chin further.

Simon knew it was pride talking and could not fault the man because of it. "I understand that, Merlin, but would also add that should you require my help at any time then my offer is always open."

Color flushed his face as he struggled to keep his mouth shut, and then he nodded abruptly. "Mighty fine of you, my lord."

"I want you wed as soon as it can be arranged, and if you or Jilly have any further trouble from any of the staff, I wish to know of it."

The door opened again and in slipped Jilly. Simon wondered how this sweet looking young woman had ever found her way into Merlin's arms. She came to his shoulder.

Slender as a reed, she had black curls and brown eyes, and her complexion was the color of a peach. She moved to Merlin's side, where he took her hand and squeezed it briefly.

"Hello, Jilly. There is no need to be afraid. Now I want to ask you a question, and I would ask that you answer me honestly, please." The girl nodded so Simon continued. "Do you wish to marry this man?"

"Oh yes, my lord." She looked up at the coachman with such adoration in her eyes, it caused Simon a pang of jealousy. To date, he could honestly say, no woman had ever looked at him that way.

"Excellent. Well then, you have my congratulations, and please let me know when you have all the details in place, Merlin."

Merlin bowed, Jilly curtsied, and then they both left the room, leaving Simon to finish his now lukewarm coffee. Bilby reappeared to remove his breakfast as he was finishing the paper.

"I want to know if there is any trouble for either Jilly or Merlin, and please pass on to both my cook and housekeeper that if there is, it will not be my maid or coachman leaving my employ, Bilby."

"I will see to it at once, my lord, and thank you."

An hour later, he was seated on his horse and making his way through London. He stopped briefly to buy flowers on the way, but it did not take him long to reach the Duke and Duchess of Stratton's house. Dismounting, he handed over his reins to Daniel's groom and then made his way to the front door. He was surprised when it opened before he knocked.

"Simon!"

"Hello, Eva," he said, "and my favorite little person." Georgia waved a pudgy fist, then lunged out of her mother's arms at him. Catching her, he pulled her close, inhaling her baby scent. Placing several loud kisses on her sweet-smelling cheek, he then whispered into her ear, which she loved. Simon adored children and babies. Little people, to his mind, were less complicated than the grown-up ones. If they were hungry or angry, they simply let you know it in a loud, demonstrative manner. They responded to him without the restraint of social restrictions, and most of all, they loved to be hugged.

"Are those for me?" Eva questioned, nodding to the flowers he held out of Georgia's reach.

"Of course."

She took them and buried her nose in the colorful blooms. "You always bring flowers and I love them, Simon. Thank you."

Taking them from her, he then handed them to the butler so he could kiss Eva's cheek. "You're welcome, darling. Are you going out?" he added, once he had the baby settled against his chest.

"Yes, we're visiting Claire and her mother, but do go on up, as grandmother is here and Daniel will be pleased of your support."

Simon visibly shuddered at the mention of Daniel's grandmother. The Dowager Duchess of Stratton was an old termagant who instilled the fear of god in all whom crossed her path, with her caustic comments and general air of ill will.

"Ah, if you don't mind, I'll accompany you, as it has been a long time since I visited Mathew Belmont." This would give him a chance to observe Claire again and maybe get her alone for a few minutes.

Eva gave studied him. "I was not aware you and Claire's brother were any more than passing acquaintants, Simon."

"Oh, Mathew and I have known each other for years,"

Simon said with a perfectly straight face. It was not strictly speaking a lie, after all, they had known of each other for years—they just rarely conversed.

"He may not be there, and then you'll have to take tea with me and Claire until I'm ready to leave."

"I'm sure Georgia will keep me company, won't you darling?"

The little girl gave him a smile that displayed one tooth and pink gums. She then grabbed his necktie and tugged.

"Very well, but you will be in no fit state to visit if you let her keep doing that," Eva said, urging him out to the carriage.

"Dare I enquire as to why, Kelkirk, you are getting into a carriage with my duchess and daughter?"

Simon looked up and saw Daniel standing on the small balcony above him. Georgia squealed when she saw her father, who, in turn, pulled a funny face.

"The better man has finally won, your grace."

"He is trying to avoid Grandmother, therefore he is accompanying me to visit Claire," Eva said from beside him.

"I thought you had the same relationship with Claire that you had with my grandmother." Daniel looked over his shoulder to make sure his elderly relation had not followed him outside.

"Claire and I are friends," Daniel said defensively as Georgia undid another fold on his necktie and then stuffed it into her mouth.

"No you're not," the duke and duchess said in unison. "In fact," Daniel added, looking smug, "I believe she said you made her feel like she was wearing a hair shirt."

"Did she say that?" Simon removed his necktie from Georgia's mouth, but she just fixed her gums on one of the buttons of his jacket.

"For pity's sake, man, everyone knows it. You two are like two stray cats when you are near each other, all hackles and hissing." The duke now leaned on the balcony, obviously enjoying his friend's discomfort.

"Rubbish," Simon said. "Claire and I are always polite to each other. We are friends."

"Polite, yes—friendly, no."

"Ah well, the rest of society loves me, Stratton, so I'm sure I shall cope without Miss Belmont's adoration."

The duke snorted at that. "I don't adore you, and I'm pretty sure my wife only tolerates you."

"Don't listen to him, Simon. Of course we both adore you." Eva patted his hand.

"Dukes do not yell in the streets, Grandson. Must I constantly remind you of your position in society? With whom are you conversing in such a loud voice?" The Dowager Duchess of Stratton appeared behind her grandson.

"He is sadly lacking in manners, your grace. Please have stern words with him whilst we depart," Simon said, acknowledging the elderly lady with a bow that made Georgia giggle as he tipped her upside down then righted her again.

"Goodbye, Grandmother," Eva said as Simon urged her into the carriage and climbed in behind her.

"Look after my women!"

Simon lifted a hand at the duke's words, and then a footman shut the door behind them.

"Lady Carmichael told me Miss Lydia Simpett has eloped, Claire. Of course her father is refuting the claim and saying she is laid low with a stomach ailment, but Lady Carmichael is quite sure of the accuracy behind the rumor."

Murmuring the appropriate response, Claire let her mother rattle on as she did most mornings at the breakfast table. Mathew, of course, was buried in the paper.

Claire had not slept well. Upon returning from the ball, she'd washed and changed into her nightdress. She'd then brushed her hair and sipped the tea Plimley had left for her, going through the preparing-for-sleep rituals she had been enacting since Anthony's death. Her bed had been turned down and the lavender scented sheets should have been inviting, yet upon climbing into bed, she had felt her body grow rigid. All tiredness had suddenly fled as thoughts bombarded her.

Relax, Claire—deep breaths, she'd reminded herself when her thoughts had gone to Anthony and what he had left in France. Closing her eyes, she had willed herself to sleep, but restfulness hadn't come, so she'd tried to occupy her mind with thoughts other than her inability to sleep. She'd counted all the people who'd worn purple at the ball, including Lady Bellwater, whose dress had been a nasty, violent shade that clashed horribly with her orange slippers. Then she'd recalled all her dance partners, of which there were many, due to her determination to avoid Simon. That thought had made her think about Simon and why he was so intent on finding out the reasons for her behavior today. Eventually, after forcing herself to lie in the dark, she had thrown back the covers and stalked from her room into the next one. Plimley had, as usual, laid the fire and placed a lamp. Choosing a book she had already read twice before, Claire then lay on the sofa and dozed and read for the remainder of the night until the sun began to rise. She had then slipped outside and walked through the gardens, inhaling the coming day and the clean fresh scent of nature. It was out there she missed her brother the most.

When Anthony was sick, they had sat in the gardens for hours, especially to watch the sun rise. She would wrap him in blankets and they would walk slowly about until, exhausted, he would sit and say, 'Go to bed now, Claire, I can manage,' to which she always shook her head and then laid it on his shoulder, and together, they would silently wait for the new day to arrive.

"You look tired this morning, Claire. Did you not sleep well?"

Pulled from her thoughts by her brother's voice, Claire looked across at Mathew. He usually never conversed in the morning—well, at least until he had finished reading his paper. She searched for her mother and noted she had left the room while Claire had been deep in thought.

"All you have said to me in the past two days, Mathew, is how tired I look," Claire said, keeping her tone light.

"Perhaps that is because you keep swallowing a yawn when you think I'm not looking."

Her family did not know she'd had trouble sleeping since Anthony's death, and why would they, as they were sleeping when she was not. Furthermore, she wasn't close enough with Mathew to confide in him. And she had no wish to worry her mother.

"More tea, Miss Belmont?"

Claire gave Plimley a grateful smile. He was always near when she needed a diversion. Her mother, she could usually distract, but Mathew tended to be more tenacious. "Thank you, Plimley, and how is Helen this morning?"

"Much better, thank you, Miss Belmont. Her headache is passing, and she should back to work tomorrow."

"Who is Helen?"

"Honestly, Mathew, Helen is one of your maids and she suffers terribly from headaches. But we seem to be getting them sorted, as this is the first in many months." Claire lifted her cup and took a sip.

"Do you know the names of all the staff here, Claire?"

Simon Kelkirk was the only other person who stared at her the way Mathew was doing right now. It was as if no one else existed at that moment. For the most, Claire avoided her brother's penetrating looks and probing questions, but occasionally, when she wasn't concentrating, he caught her out.

"Yes, Mathew, I do."

He eyes held hers. "You haven't answered my question little sister. Are you tired this morning?"

"Of course I'm tired, Mathew. I danced until my feet hurt and did not find my bed till well past midnight."

"Before he died Anthony told me he was worried about you because you had stopped sleeping since he returned, as you insisted on caring for him during the night. He feared that with his death this would not change. Is that the case, Claire, do you struggle to sleep?"

His question surprised her, as they rarely mentioned their brother. The subject was too painful for both of them.

"Claire?"

"Why are you asking me this now when he has been dead many years?" Claire kept her eyes on the plate before her. "All this brotherly concern is quite overwhelming," she added, keeping her tone light.

"Because he also told me you needed watching, and to my lasting regret, I have provided for you but perhaps not watched over you as well as I should have."

Claire gripped the sides of her chair hard as she looked up at the concern in his eyes. Why now did he want to play the big brother when before, he was indifferent to her?

"I am all grown up now, Mathew. There is no need for this, I assure you. We are not like that, you and I—"

"Like what, Claire? Close, do you mean, as you were with Anthony?"

She had told Anthony everything. There had been moments since their brother's death in which Claire had needed Mathew. She'd wanted him to hold her and tell her everything would be all right and that the pain of missing

Anthony would ease, but he had never been there for her, and perhaps she had not been there for him, either. It was too late now, of course, to establish that kind of relationship.

"I am not sure why we are having this conversation now, Mathew." She wanted to look away from his intense gaze, yet could not do so. It was almost as if he was willing her to keep the contact with him.

"I hope you would come to me if you had a problem, Claire."

"What problem could I possibly have, Mathew? My life is exactly as it should be." Again, she was subjected to a long, silent look.

"And yet you received a note yesterday, delivered to the servant's entrance, and then you left the house without your maid."

Dear god!

"I want to know what was in that note, sister."

"I-It was just a note from a friend in need, Mathew. Nothing nefarious, I assure you," Claire said with a dismissive wave of her hand. Who had told him?

"What are you two talking about?"

Dragging her eyes from her brother, Claire looked gratefully at her mother as she walked back into the room. Forcing herself to let go of the chair, she reached for her cup of lukewarm tea. "Mathew was telling me his eggs were cold," Claire said before taking a sip.

"Well, perhaps if he had eaten them when they were hot instead of burrowing into the paper, he would have enjoyed them more."

"Thank you, Mother, I had not thought of that."

Claire knew she should have told Mathew about the note. However, she hadn't because it had singled her out, and said not to tell anyone. She also believed that whatever Anthony had left behind was very important, and Claire wanted nothing to hinder her chances of retrieving it.

"Are Eva and the baby still coming for a visit this morning, Claire?"

"Indeed they are, Mother, and I had best get ready to greet them," Claire said, rising. "Excuse me."

Mathew's eyes followed her from the room, and Claire was glad to close the door behind her. One of the staff must have told him about the note, and like Simon, Mathew was tenacious and would ask her until she told him what it had said.

"Lord, what a conundrum," Claire muttered as she made her way back to her room. Her life had been so simple just a few days ago, and now she had the note, Simon, and Mathew to contend with. Her maid helped her change and prepare for Eva's visit, and she applied more powder, then pinched her cheeks, hard.

"The Duchess of Stratton has arrived, Miss Belmont."

"Thank you, Plimley," Eva called through the door.

Claire made her way down the stairs to where Eva and Georgia were waiting. The smile on her face was now genuine. She had fallen in love with the little cherub, and at least for a few hours, she could be herself, chat and laugh with her best friend and mother without a brooding male questioning her. Hurrying inside the parlor she came to an abrupt halt.

CHAPTER FOUR

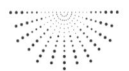

Simon was standing by the windows with Georgia in his arms. He was having a conversation with Mathew, and both men seemed oblivious to the fact that the little girl had undone Simon's necktie and was sucking on it.

"Hello, Claire."

Dragging her eyes from the picture Simon presented and forcing the smile back onto her face, Claire hurried to greet her friend.

"Simon insisted on accompanying me when he heard Grandmother was visiting with Daniel. You know how she terrifies him."

Claire kissed Eva's cheek and tried not to look at Simon.

"You don't mind, do you?"

Yes, she shrieked silently. "Of course not."

"You had best go and give Georgia a kiss, Claire. She has noticed your arrival."

The little girl was waving her hands about and making noises while looking at Claire, who in turn did not want to go anywhere near the male holding her or her brother.

"Go now, before she starts squealing." Eva gave Claire a little nudge, which sent her reluctantly on her way.

She curtsied to Simon, avoiding his eyes as he stopped speaking to Mathew, and looked at her. She then took one of the hands Georgia was waving about. "Hello, sweetheart, how are you today?"

"Very well, darling, and you?"

The deep words were whispered in her ear as Mathew turned to speak to a footman. Ignoring them and the small shiver they produced inside her, Claire leaned forward and kissed the baby's cheek.

"She likes it if you make disgusting noises whilst you kiss her."

"I don't make disgusting noises, Lord Kelkirk," Claire said in a prim voice that made her sound like her mother. She wanted to take the child from him, yet did not want to ask.

"What? Never? How very controlled you are, Miss Belmont."

She refused to acknowledge those words or any meaning behind them, so she ignored him and ran a finger down the baby's soft cheek.

"Please excuse me for a moment. There is a matter I must attend to."

Simon and Claire nodded to Mathew, and then he left the room with the footman at his heels. At least one of her problems had gone.

"I like to be in control." Claire knew she sounded defensive, yet couldn't help herself.

"Surely there are times when you can let someone else take up the reins?"

She always felt he was saying one thing and meaning another. The man was very taxing to converse with. "I prefer to handle my own reins, thank you, my lord." Claire took the tiny fist Georgia waved at her and opened the fingers to press a kiss on her palm.

"I have quite a steady hand on the reins, so I've been told, should you need to share."

Blowing out a frustrated breath, Claire looked up into his twinkling grey eyes. "Can you never be serious?"

He did not answer straightaway, and Claire held her breath as she waited for a response.

"If you'll remember last night, Claire, I was very serious."

Babies presented the perfect opportunity to avoid answering difficult questions, so Claire ignored Simon and began to tickle Georgia under the chin until the little girl gurgled back at her.

"It constantly amazes me that such a small creature can captivate a room full of adults. She is a constant delight, isn't she? I swear she holds my heart right there in that tiny palm."

The sincerity behind his words touched Claire, and for that brief moment as they looked at Georgia, she knew they were of one mind. This little girl meant so much to both of them.

"It is no different for me, my lord."

"I know," he said and then handed her Georgia. "Don't you think it grossly unfair that when she belches, moves her bowel, or makes a lot of noise, everyone applauds, telling her what a good baby she has been, yet if I did the same I would be run out of town?"

Claire had always kept her distance from Simon Kelkirk because there was something about him that unsettled her. He wasn't like other men; he didn't observe the correct distance when conversing or dancing with a woman, nor did he guard his tongue. In fact, he was the opposite of everything she strove to be, and she had never known how to handle him. He was a favorite to many. Perhaps because of his uniqueness and perhaps because everything he did was usually accompanied by a smile. Whatever the reason, he seemed unable to do wrong in the eyes of society.

Their relationship had started with her provoking him, and never really progressed beyond that. He was to her like the stable master's son had been growing up. He had thrown things at her, pushed her over and generally tormented her, and because she had thought him the most handsome boy she had ever seen, she had done the same back. Of course, she didn't think Lord Kelkirk the most handsome man she'd ever seen; he just produced the same reactions in her.

"I hardly think that is something we should discuss on a morning call, Lord Kelkirk."

He studied her so thoroughly that Claire held her breath again, and then he bent down and spoke to the baby. "Aunty Claire will be gentle with you, Georgie. It's just men she doesn't like."

"I…I do so like men!" Claire spluttered, clamping a hand over the baby's ears.

She was subjected to another steady look. "So it's just me you don't like, then. I had wondered."

Claire had worked hard over the years at not losing her composure. She rarely blushed. The few times she had, she'd been in this man's company. She hated the heat that stole into her cheeks at his words now. It suggested he could unsettle her, which obviously, he did. "Perhaps if you were not hell-bent on provoking me, we would not constantly be at each other's throats," she snapped, ignoring the heat in her cheeks. "And my name is Miss Belmont."

He gave her a wide smile that showed off his white teeth and made him look far too handsome. Horrid beast. He knew what his smile did to a woman—not her, of course, but the more foolish of her sex.

"Is that your way of telling me that if I was nicer, you would like me, Claire?"

"I neither like nor dislike you, Lord Kelkirk. We are acquaintances."

Suddenly he looked serious. His eyes lost their friendly sparkle, a sight she had rarely seen.

"I had hoped we were friends, Claire. Friends who are there for each other, should we be required."

She suddenly felt warm all over, as if him saying he was there for her had lit a torch inside her and was heating all those places that had never been warm before. "Don't… please." Claire stumbled over the words as she looked down at Georgia nestled against her.

"Don't what, Claire? Tell your brother I saw you in a distressed state yesterday and you will not tell me why? I'm concerned for you—can't you understand that?"

The baby must have felt the tension between them, as she started to fuss. Lifting her over her shoulder, Claire rubbed Georgia's back. How did she answer him?

"There is nothing wrong with me, Lord Kelkirk, and the reasons I was there are mine alone. Now if you will excuse me, I have neglected Eva for too long." She hurried to sit next to the duchess, who did not notice her agitation, having eyes only for the child she instantly took onto her lap. Ignoring Simon as he moved to take the seat beside her, Claire started to chat about the previous night's engagement until tea arrived.

"How do you take your tea, Lord Kelkirk?" Claire said, looking down at the pot in her hands.

"Milk and sugar, Claire." He said her name slowly, drawing out the single syllable to make it sound as though it had four. "And I will take one of those biscuits. Perhaps two," he added.

Claire placed the cup and plate on the small table to his right.

"You are, indeed, kindness itself, Miss Belmont."

"And you are bloody irritating," she hissed before she could stop herself. His laughter followed her back to her seat.

"Daniel has been called to Stratton, Claire, and I have decided to accompany him. We are to leave in three days."

"How long will you be gone?" Claire said, looking at her friend. She would miss her dearly, and her daughter, too.

"Only a week or two but I had wondered if you would like to accompany us? Daniel thinks the rest will do you good."

Claire replaced her cup on its saucer slowly. "Why does he think I need a rest?"

"He said he caught you yawning several times behind your hand last night, and that you had smudges beneath your eyes, if one got close enough to notice."

He hadn't said anything, but she felt the intensity of Simon's gaze as Eva spoke. Whereas before he'd been listening with one ear while his mind had seemed to wander, as most men's did when women gossiped, now he was focused fully on the conversation she and the duchess were having.

"I had not realized I looked so haggard." Claire's words sounded high pitched. She could feel the panic growing inside her. First Simon and Mathew, now Daniel. Had anyone else seen the smudges and yawns?

"Now, darling, you know that's not true—it is simply that Daniel knows you better than most and was concerned."

Claire took the hand Eva held out to her and squeezed it briefly. "I'm sorry, and, yes, I have been a bit weary. Perhaps the break is just what I need. However I will need to ask mother first—"

"Ask mother what?" Lady Belmont sailed across the room. She wore her favorite color of blue, and her hair was immaculately arranged. As usual, she presented an elegant picture. Her smile widened as she saw Georgia. "Give me that baby at once!"

"The duke and duchess are going to the country for a few days and wished my company on their travels, Mother." Claire realized she really did want to leave London with her friends. In the country she could breathe easier without anyone looking over her shoulder.

Lady Belmont picked up Georgia and took the seat beside Simon as Claire poured her tea.

"We have just received an invitation for the Botheringham house party, which is in three weeks, so perhaps a break now will do you good, Daughter. I think you should go with them and this delightful child."

Claire felt her heart sink to her toes. House parties were horrible for her because if she was having a sleepless night, she was confined to her room in case other guests came across her wandering the halls in the early hours of the morning.

"We are all going to the Botheringham's, aren't we, Simon?" Eva said. "Lady Botheringham has asked that I bring Georgia, too."

"I can hardly contain my excitement," Simon drawled, looking at Claire.

Why, after so long in his acquaintance, was she struggling to find her usual poise? *Because he saw you in that lane and he suspects something, although he's not sure what.* Everything had changed between them now, because he knew she had a secret. Of course she didn't know what that secret was yet… but she would, he however, would not.

There was only one way to deter Simon and his suspicions, and that was to throw him off the scent. To do that, Claire needed to do what she always had. Provoke and challenge him, make him think of something other than seeing her in that lane.

"Of course you can barely contain your excitement, Lord Kelkirk—there will be everything you love at that house party."

Simon uncrossed his knees and braced his hands on them, giving her his undivided attention. Grey eyes fixed on her face, he said, "And what do I love, Claire?"

Me. Claire had no idea where that thought came from and quickly banished it as ridiculous. "Flirtations, food, and attention."

Eva and her mother laughed, as she had meant them to.

"You think you know me so well, Miss Belmont?"

He was smiling, yet his eyes were still serious, and Claire realized that in fact she didn't know much about him other than the persona she saw in public. She knew he was the most loyal of friends to Eva and Daniel, and that he would protect both of them and their daughter with whatever means it took, but what else was there to this man?

"Of course." Claire forced a laugh. "Have I not witnessed your behavior almost nightly for the past few years?"

More laughter, but not from him. He just gave her a gentle smile. "I hope there is a bit more substance to me than that."

"Of course there is, Simon," Eva soothed. "Other than my husband, you are the most wonderful man I know. Some woman will be extremely lucky to have you as her husband one day."

"Thank you, darling, and I assure you, that you are first equal in my affections, also," he drawled.

"And who is the other lucky recipient of your adoration, Lord Kelkirk?"

Claire held her breath as she waited for him to answer her mother's question. Had he given his heart to someone? Was he about to declare his intention to wed?

"My aunt," he said with a knowing smile, almost as if he had guessed her thoughts.

"It is time you married, my lord. Perhaps I may offer a few suggestions to you?"

"Mother, I don't think—"

Simon held up one hand. "I would love to hear your mother's suggestions, Claire. After all, I am not getting any younger, and she is a woman of great sense and discerning tastes… unlike her daughter."

The last was said so softly that only Claire heard it. "I have great sense!"

"Pardon, dear?"

Claire waved her hand about and then gave Simon a foul look, which he returned with a smug smile.

"Miss Tarlton," Lady Belmont said. "Her family is highly regarded, and she has pleasing manners, Lord Kelkirk."

"Too tame for me, I'm afraid. I cannot have a wife who will trot about obeying my every command, Lady Belmont. As your daughter will tell you, I am already conceited."

There was silence after this. Even Georgia appeared to be pondering the situation.

"Miss Stamford. She is beautiful and sweet-natured, yet has a strength to her personality that I am sure you will find pleasing, Lord Kelkirk."

He replaced his cup carefully before answering, and Claire found herself leaning forward, eager to hear what he would say.

"I could not sit across the breakfast table and bask in such unblemished beauty day after day, my lady. Miss Stamford has no flaws. Even the tone of her voice is melodious. Alas, I am a severely blemished man and could not hope to compete."

"Now you're just toying with me, my lord." Claire watched her mother titter.

"Indeed, I am not, as my years are progressing, and matrimony is most definitely a consideration soon." He looked at Claire again, his eyes running over her face before returning to her mother. "I will marry, Lady Belmont, but the woman I marry will be the partner of my choice, as I plan to spend the remainder of my days in her company."

"Men always say such things, Lord Kelkirk," her mother scoffed. "But inevitably, they find their clubs and other arenas of pleasure."

Claire shot her mother a surprised look. She rarely spoke so candidly and never in company. Lady Belmont was jiggling Georgia but looking at Simon, her eyes deadly serious.

"Mother—"

"It's all right, Claire. Your mother and I are well acquainted, and she can speak freely with me. In fact, I appreciate a woman who speaks her mind," Simon said, nodding to Lady Belmont. "And I will add that my wife will never have cause to question my fealty to her. She will be the only woman with whom I share my home and heart."

Claire heard her mother say something, yet she did not know what, as her head was filled with Simon's words. *She will be the only woman with whom I share my home and heart.* He had sounded sincere, each word spoken carefully, and she had believed him, even though she had often labeled him a carefree rake.

"Yes, what is it, Plimley?" Claire questioned the butler as he appeared at her side.

"Lord Belmont has received urgent correspondence, which he would like to share with you at once, Miss Belmont."

Claire wasn't sure why, but her heart suddenly started to thump rapidly in her chest.

"And we must leave, as it is time for Georgia's nap." Eva rose and took the baby from Lady Belmont.

"Tell my brother I will be with him shortly, Plimley," Claire said, regaining her feet, too. Why was she suddenly so tense? Yes, Mathew had rarely asked her opinion on things, but that did not mean he couldn't now.

"I shall claim a dance tonight, Claire," Simon said, taking her hand and bowing deeply before he escorted Eva and the baby out to the waiting carriage. It was as she closed the door behind them that she realized she had not answered him.

With her mind conjuring up possibilities of why Mathew wished to see her, Claire slowly made her way to her brother's study. Did he wish to question her further about her sleeplessness?

Tapping on the door, she opened it. "You wished to see me, Mathew?"

"Yes. Come in and close the door, Claire."

She did as he asked and then took the seat across from his desk.

"Read this." He thrust a note across the desktop toward her, his fingers Claire noticed, were trembling. His face was pale and drawn, and she almost snatched her hand back as she reached for the paper. Something inside her dreaded reading the words written upon it. Taking a deep breath, she lifted the missive and began to read. Seconds later, the paper fluttered from her fingers as she slumped backward into the chair.

CHAPTER FIVE

"Was that Belmont striding past us looking fierce?" Simon watched as the man stalked across the street ahead of him.

"Where?"

"Having trouble focusing, your grace?" Simon said, pointing at the rapidly disappearing figure of Claire's brother. Well, he thought it was Claire's brother. "I believe there is an ocular specialist further up the street. If you'll take my arm, I'll escort you there."

Daniel muttered something foul before following the direction of Simon's hand. "My vision is superb, as you very well know, Kelkirk," he snapped.

"I'm sure that was Belmont," Simon said again. "He was certainly in a hurry."

"And why do you care if it was?" Daniel said as they started walking toward the tavern they often frequented. "To the best of my knowledge, you've only ever conversed with the man in social situations. Therefore you can hardly know if he scowls daily or not."

"If you'll step to the left, your grace, you'll avoid landing in that pile of steaming horse excrement."

"I can see it!" Daniel snapped. "My vision is near perfect, for god's sake!"

"Of course it is." Simon always enjoyed taunting his friend.

"I'm going to carve you up after we've eaten, Kelkirk. I have a new foil that needs a workout, and you will not be quite so ready with your insults after that."

"I have spoken more than two words to Belmont," Simon said, knowing Daniel would follow his conversational leaps. After all, they had been friends for years. "When I visited Claire with your beautiful wife and daughter, he was there. In fact, we talked for some time."

"Still, I don't believe I've heard you show any interest in the man before today."

Simon opened the tavern door and motioned for Daniel to enter before following. They walked into the dark interior and headed to the booth they usually occupied. Creatures of habit, Eva often called him and Daniel.

"Did you notice that the Belmont family have not attended any social engagements for two nights?" Simon added.

"And I repeat, why the interest in Belmont?" the duke demanded.

"Hello, my lovely lords."

The blonde waitress had a smile as big as her ample breasts and had served them for as long as they'd been coming to her establishment. They'd never corrected her, or added that Simon was the lord and Daniel was a duke. If she wanted to call them her lovely lords, then who were they to dissuade her? Besides, the only word that really went well with duke, Simon often pointed out, was dirty.

"Still the most beautiful woman in the United Kingdom, Lottie," Simon said.

"Tis not only you that notices, my lord," she pushed out her breasts.

"Just the usual, please, Lottie," Daniel said, rolling his eyes at Simon and sending the waitress on her way.

"Before you were committed to wedded bliss, Stratton, you enjoyed flirting, too, so please do not spoil it for those of us still in the unmarried state."

Daniel leant back in the booth and looked at Simon. "As Eva called us creatures of habit, I have ordered beef and vegetable instead of rabbit."

"Well, that's telling her," Simon said, looking around the dim interior. They'd been coming here since they'd first come to London over ten years ago. Not much had changed. In fact, he was sure the man slumped over the bar was a permanent fixture.

"Eva said Claire sent a note around saying she was sick, and that's why you've not seen her the past two evenings."

"Sick? What kind of sick?" Simon demanded, suddenly feeling cold all over.

"A headache, I believe."

Lottie placed their food before them with two large ales, and Simon could not dredge up his usual leer as she gave him an eyeful of her splendid breasts. How the hell was Simon supposed to eat with a big lump in his throat?

"Something's not right there," he blurted out before he could stop himself. They were best friends, and Simon had never had secrets from Daniel. Besides, he needed to talk to someone.

"What's not right where?" The duke picked up his ale and downed half of it.

"Claire. Something's off with her. I'm sure of it."

"You're showing a great deal of interest in the Belmont

family, and most especially a woman you cannot be within two feet off without a verbal debate erupting."

"That's of her making, not mine." Simon felt moved to defend himself.

Snorting, Daniel picked up his fork and then pointed it at Simon. "Do you know, I think you could be right about Claire. I told Eva she looked out of sorts just the other day."

Simon was sure he could eat around the lump. After all, someone had gone to the trouble of baking the pie; the least he could do was eat it. Sinking his teeth into the soft pastry, he let out a few humming noises of appreciation. "I want to tell you something, but you have to keep it to yourself," he said after he'd swallowed.

"I don't have secrets from my wife, Simon. You know that."

"All right, you can tell, Eva, but not Georgia. She's a terrible gossip."

The duke grunted.

Simon ate more pie and drank more ale while he thought about what to say, and Daniel did the same, watching Simon's every mouthful.

"I'll give you two more minutes, and then I'm pummeling it out of you," Daniel said, once again pointing his fork at Simon.

"Didn't your father spend a considerable amount of money teaching you not to wave your cutlery around whilst eating, your grace?"

"One minute."

"I was just getting the words right in my head."

"The annoying habit you have of thinking everything through before you speak has long since lost its charm for me, Kelkirk. Therefore I beseech you in this instance to speak the first words that come into your head." Daniel once again slouched back in his seat, ale in hand.

"Tsk tsk. Slouching, too, your Grace."

"Remember that I have a new rapier, Kelkirk. It would not pay you to antagonize me."

"When I was late for our lunch meeting at the club the other day, it was because I bumped into Claire… literally." Simon went on to tell Daniel about his meeting with Claire and subsequent sore jaw.

"Good god!" The duke looked stunned. "And you have no idea why she was there?"

"None, and when I questioned her, she looked scared, Daniel, and that was more worrying, as to the best of my knowledge, nothing scares Claire Belmont. In fact, she is always just so."

"Just so what?"

"Composed, immaculately attired, well spoken—you name it." Simon waved his hand around.

"She wasn't always," Daniel said quietly. "There was a time when she was wild and unruly, and then her brother died."

"Anthony?"

The duke nodded, his face solemn. "He was everything to Claire. There were four years between them, and unlike Mathew, who had duties ahead of him, Anthony always had time for Claire, and she adored him. We were friends, all three of us, and we used to run wild through the pastures of our homes. Claire was younger, of course, and although we tried to leave her behind, she always found us, and because Anthony loved her so much, he let her stay." Simon watched the emotions move across his friend's face as he remembered. "And then he went away to war and got wounded and when he returned, like so many, he was a changed man."

"He died five years ago, I believe?"

The duke nodded. "Six months after returning home, he was dead."

"Yes, and it was Claire who nursed him to the end.

"Simon could imagine her sitting at her brother's bedside for hours doing all the things that he needed with endless patience. He'd seen her compassion with others and the tender way she was with Georgia. It was just him she was impatient with.

"Her mother told me, when I called to inquire after Anthony, that he did not sleep—couldn't sleep—as the pain in his side was too much to bear. The bullet was lodged inside, and the doctors said if they removed it, he would die."

"But he died, anyway," Simon added softly. "And Claire lost the brother she loved most."

Daniel looked into the depths of his drink before speaking. "I had drifted away from her by then. I had you and our friends," he added, shooting Simon a look to make sure he understood. "I called to see her, but she didn't want to see me, and I tried once more, but she was still deeply upset, so I left her alone. It was only after I married Eva that we became re-acquainted."

They were silent for a while as they both thought about Claire, each in their own way, and what she had suffered.

"Daniel, Claire knows you are her friend and always have been, and now you have given her Eva, too. I would not feel too badly for what has been."

"I hope you're right, Simon, and now we need to think more on why she was in that street and how to go about getting the information from her."

"You're taking her to Stratton, so that would be as good a time as any to start questioning her, Daniel."

The duke nodded. "Eva can get the information from her. She only has to smile and people usually tell her everything."

"Besotted fool," Simon said with no malice, and Daniel smiled.

Rising, the duke put some coins on the table. "Come, I

need to think about his some more, and as I do my best thinking while I'm moving, it's time to teach you a lesson in fencing."

Snorting, Simon followed him out the door. The day had grown darker as rain clouds threatened, and he guessed by nightfall there would be a deluge, which would turn the streets to sludge. Shuddering at the thought, he fell in beside Daniel as they made their way across the road.

He felt better for having told Daniel his concerns. Now his friend could help Simon to find out what was going on with Claire and why she had been in that lane. He just hoped that whatever it turned out to be, they could find a way to resolve it for her. Because he could not bear the thought of Claire Belmont suffering with either a broken heart or body.

CHAPTER SIX

Claire looked out her bedroom window at the grey skies over London. She had not left the house for two days, and in that time the rain had steadily fallen and was showing no appearance of letting up. It wasn't overly cold, yet she had a shawl over her shoulders, and a permanent chill seemed to have taken up residence in her body. Looking at her bed, she contemplated lying down—just closing her eyes to seek some relief from the thoughts inside her head, if only for a while. Exhaustion had long since passed, and now Claire was beyond simple tiredness. Rubbing her eyes, she took a deep, steadying breath. Becoming weepy helped no one, least of all the child who now needed her.

"Who is it?" Claire said as a knock sounded at the door.

"Mathew."

"Go away." Claire's voice had not risen. It was flat and raw, yet she knew her brother had heard her words, even though he'd chosen to ignore them. She hurried to the window seat, and sat as the handle turned and he entered. "I believe I asked you to go away." She wrapped her arms around her knees and hugged them close to her chest.

"What you did the other day was irresponsible and could easily have turned out badly, Claire. You should have come to me the instant you received that note, not gone to that lane alone. I want your word you will not contemplate anything as foolish again."

Her brother looked like hell. His eyes were bloodshot, his hair stood on end, and his skin was pale, yet she felt no sympathy for him; what she felt was anger. "Don't lecture me on responsibilities, brother, when you are failing in yours."

"I am not failing in mine," he ground out. "In fact, just the opposite. Why will you not see reason on this, Claire? Mother is on my side."

"Reason!" Claire was amazed she could still find the strength to raise her voice. "Is it not reasonable to expect that we depart immediately for Liverpool to inquire if the child the note spoke of is our brother's? The brother we both loved, Mathew? Furthermore, do not use Mother to strengthen your cause—she would never go against your wishes."

His teeth snapped together briefly, and the anger between them seemed to fill every corner in her room. "The note that I intercepted was for you, Claire, and it stated you must come alone to collect Anthony's illegitimate child. If there is indeed a child, why would it matter which one of us went to retrieve it? Surely you are not silly enough to believe this ruse?"

"What if it's not, Mathew? What if Anthony's child is left alone and helpless because you will do nothing?"

"And what if someone has targeted you, wants to abduct you to obtain money? Surely you can see I must protect us from that? It was you who was lured into Tuttle Lane, not me, and it is you whom they want in Liverpool. Open your eyes and see what is happening here!"

Claire ignored his words. She believed there was a child and would do whatever she could to save it.

"We do not have long, Mathew. The note said they had Anthony's child, and they asked for me specifically because Anthony had given them my name. They will hold the child for seven days, and if after that we have not come, then he or she will be abandoned." Claire clenched her fingers together. She did not want her brother to see them trembling. Her heart started thumping again at the prospect of her niece or nephew being left cold and alone on the streets of Liverpool. "Our blood, Mathew—yours and mine."

"A bastard and more than likely a French bastard, at that, not that I believe it exists!"

The words were roared at her and hung in the air between them as they glared at each other. They had never spoken to each other this way before. Usually their conversations were polite and distant. But she would not be frightened by his anger, as she was angry, too.

"There is no child, Claire. No niece or nephew carrying your beloved brother's blood. Surely, you can see this is some kind of lure to get money from us?"

Claire wouldn't see it because she believed otherwise. There was a child. "You say you want to protect me, but what you really fear is that there will be a child, Mathew, and it will bring shame to your name."

"If there was a child," Mathew spat his words out in an angry volley, "I would of course acknowledge it in some way, however, there is no child, therefore, I refuse to discuss this further."

"Some way? Surely you would acknowledge it as your niece or nephew, Mathew? This child is something that is part of our brother. Anthony deserves more than this from you, and his child deserves our protection when its father is not here to give it."

Mathew walked in a circle around her room, pacing like a caged animal. A large hand raked continuously through his hair.

"There is no child, Claire, now I beg of you to let the matter drop. Mother is distressed, and you are making more of this mess than needs to be."

"We are discussing a small, helpless child, Mathew, not a mess."

His jaw was clenched so tight, she could see the taut muscles.

"You told me you would have someone look into it, at least, Mathew. Surely if the existence of the child is confirmed, you will go and collect it?"

He wouldn't look at her, and Claire realized with dawning horror that he had lied.

"I have said my final words on this matter, Claire. Therefore you will not speak of it again."

"Dear god, you lied to me!" Claire was suddenly filled with rage. An uncontrollable need to lash out at Mathew gripped her. "No one has been sent to Liverpool, have they? How can you do this?

"Enough! Not one more word, Claire." Anger had him stalking toward her.

Claire rose to meet him, her rage more than equaling his. "How dare you not care for our brother's child! You are a bloody coward, Mathew, concerned only for yourself and what others will think of the high and mighty Lord Belmont."

"Shut up!"

"Anthony would have done this for you, were your roles reversed, Mathew. He would not have hesitated."

His laugh was brittle as he stopped just inches from her.

"Ah, but your sainted Anthony could never do any wrong in your eyes, Claire, could he?"

"He is your brother." Claire heard the pleading in her words. "It matters not whether I believed him a saint or not—what matters is the child." Her heart sank as she saw his expression become emotionless once more. He returned to the composed Lord Belmont. "I never thought you a hard man, Mathew, or a cruel one, but this—what you are not doing—will change everything between us." Claire's words were a whisper, and in them was a final, desperate plea to her big brother for him to help her, help the child.

"You always cared more for him than me, sister. I knew that, and in truth, you have been cold and distant to me since his death. I cannot see that your future behavior will be much different."

Claire knew then she had hurt him by turning away from him when Anthony died.

"I'm sorry. I see now that my closeness to Anthony was unfair to you, but believe me, I never meant to hurt you, Mathew—"

He waved her words away. "It matters not. What matters is that I forbid any more discussion about a child that does not exist, Claire, and I will hear no more on the matter. You will go to the country tomorrow with the Duke and Duchess of Stratton, as I know they will watch over you and it will be good to remove you from London. When you return, you will not leave the house without telling me where you are going and with whom. I will know your movements every minute of every day until I'm sure that you will not put yourself in danger following this foolish hoax again."

"Surely you can't mean what you say, Mathew?" Claire stared at his unyielding face in horror.

"I mean every word. Now prepare yourself for this

evening, please. We are to leave in one hour for the Duke and Duchess of Waverly's musical."

"You expect us to go out tonight after everything that has happened?"

"That is exactly what I expect, and you will be ready and looking your best at the appointed time, or I shall force you into clothing myself."

Claire looked at the man before her. Suddenly he felt like a stranger. "I don't even know you anymore." Her words were a ragged whisper.

"Anymore," he scoffed. "You never knew me." The door slammed at his hand, and then she was alone.

Claire had no idea that the closeness between her and Anthony had upset Mathew so much. He had never seemed to care what either of them thought; he was always too busy being head of the family. Dear god, had he been lonely? Pushing aside these thoughts, she rang for her maid. She had no time now to think about Mathew, and after what she was about to do tomorrow, they would probably never speak again. Therefore there was nothing to be gained by getting herself worked up about it. He had ordered her appearance this evening, and she did not want to antagonize him further because he was still allowing her to go to Stratton, and as this was her only chance to do what she must, she would appease him until she left.

She would need to look her best, and to do that, she would need a great deal of time and careful application of face powders and such. Summoning her maid, Claire set to work. An hour later, she studied her reflection in the mirror and knew she looked as good as she could, considering the shadows beneath her eyes. Her dress was peach silk, cut wide at the neck, and rested on her shoulders, displaying more of her chest than she normally showed. The sleeves were short and fitted, as was the bodice, and a thin, matching ribbon banded tightly beneath her breasts. The skirts were light and fine, dancing around her legs as she walked. Any other evening, she would simply enjoy wearing this beautiful dress, however tonight it would provide the armor she required to draw attention away from her face. Her hair was soft, with long curls teased to lie on her shoulders. She wore a gold bracelet and thin necklace but no other jewels. She had no wish to wear anything her family had given her.

She presented herself in the hallway at the time her brother stated.

"You look lovely, dear."

Claire just nodded to her mother, who also looked lovely. Her deep rose dress was offset with rubies at her neck. Mathew looked nothing like the man who had paced around her room an hour ago. He, too, was dressed elegantly, with a waistcoat of emerald and ivory satin, a fitted black jacket, and white evening trousers.

"Claire, we must talk more about this—"

"There is a child of our blood who needs us, and you and Mathew have turned your backs on it, Mother. What more is there to say?" *Damn*, she had been determined not to discuss this again tonight.

"Do not use that tone with your mother, Claire." Mathew took her arm as he spoke.

She had to try once more to reason with him. "I'm sorry, Mathew, more sorry than I can say if Anthony and I hurt you with our closeness but surely—"

"Leave it alone, Claire."

Mathew's words were a low growl, but she was not deterred. She had to plead with him to send someone to Liverpool, before she was forced to take action herself.

"I'm begging you to send someone to Liverpool, Mathew—"

"Be quiet!" The roared words echoed through the hallway. "Not one more word do you hear me?"

His fingers bit into her arm as he spoke, but she shook him free as anger flooded through her once more. "Go to hell!"

Ignoring her mother's outraged gasp, Claire sailed out the front door, where Plimley awaited with an umbrella. She gave him a brief smile and then walked with him to the carriage. "Thank you, Plimley."

He knew better than to comment upon what he had just witnessed; after all, he was the family butler. Indeed, all he said was, "Enjoy your evening, Miss Belmont."

Claire swallowed the swell of hysterical laughter. There would be no enjoyment tonight; the evening would be an exercise in survival and nothing more. She would smile, talk, and dance, then she would return to her room and work through her plan once more.

"Claire, I cannot believe you spoke to your brother in such an insulting manner. It is not like you to be so vulgar. Mathew is simply trying to do what is best for the family," Lady Belmont said as they entered the carriage.

"I will not apologize for saying what I did. It is obvious I have not been consulted or my wishes taken into consideration with regards to Anthony's child. Therefore, please do not bring the matter up again."

"Claire—"

"Leave it, Mother. Perhaps one day she will grow up," Mathew said.

Clenching her hands into fists, Claire forced her nails into the palms of her hands. It wasn't overly painful, as she was wearing gloves, but the small sting helped her to focus. Nothing further would be gained by continuing this discussion with either her mother or Mathew. Her best course of action now was to keep quiet. Thankfully, her mother followed her lead. However Claire could feel their eyes on her as she stared out the window until they reached their destination.

The Belmont's walked into the ball with smiles on their faces. If anyone had looked closely, they would have seen the strain on each, yet no one looked closely; the façade was all that mattered on occasions such as these. There was too much noise for meaningful conversation.

"I shall be with my friends."

Claire ignored her mother but heard Mathew murmur something she did not catch. Walking with no destination in mind, Claire hoped she could find someone to sit with who was as far away from her family as possible.

Chairs were set in rows before the stage, where a piano awaited a pianist. Behind it was a large vase of bright blooms, several candelabras with tall white tapers, and a black curtain. The night would be long, but at least she could sit quietly for most of it and pretend to listen to whomever performed.

"Lord Belmont, it is a pleasure to see you again. Why, Mary was just asking after you. And Miss Belmont is here with you also."

Claire had not realized Mathew was still at her back until she felt him move to her side.

"Lady Blake, it is a pleasure to see you again also," Mathew said, bowing deeply before the prune-faced woman. Claire had always loathed her and wasn't overly enamored with her daughters, either.

"Lady Blake." Claire moved closer to her brother's side. She may not have liked him very much at that moment, but he was still her blood, and although her future would probably not hold him in it, she would not see him shackled to one of the Blake sisters.

"Miss Belmont, that is a rather…dashing dress."

Claire held still with a bored expression on her face as Lady Blake looked her over with a curl to her lips. The woman had gall—she'd give her that—especially as she herself usually wore gowns so low-cut, most people held their breath when she leant forward.

"Why, thank you, my lady. Coming from an arbiter of fashion such as yourself, that is a compliment indeed."

"Lord Belmont, I declare my evening is now complete. Mother, shame on you for monopolizing the most handsome man in the room." Lavinia Blake pushed in front of her mother to give Mathew a suggestive smile followed by a little giggle that made her exposed breasts wiggle. She was the nastiest of the three Blake sisters, probably as she was the oldest and had sharpened her claws longer than the other two. She gave Claire's gown a dismissive glance, then returned her gaze to Mathew. Her eyes narrowed as she calculated how best to capture his attention. "I have heard there may be dancing later, my lord. I hope you will partner me at least once, if not twice."

In the normal course of an evening, Claire would simply dismiss Lavinia Blake's forward behavior. She would usually just shrug and offer the girl a platitude, then move on to someone who did not annoy her quite as much. However since her brother had informed her they would not be going to Liverpool for Anthony's child, she had been seething with unsuppressed rage. Unfortunately for the foolish girl, Claire needed an outlet for some of that anger, and she was about to be the recipient.

"But surely to dance twice would cause speculation, Miss Blake." Claire smiled but not sweetly. "A lady such as you, barely out in society, should not risk censure from those of us who are more experienced." Leaning forward in what appeared to be a friendly manner, she then tapped the girl's hand, and she was fairly sure her eyes shot flames as Lavinia

Blake stepped back onto her mother's foot. "Furthermore, Miss Blake, the man should always do the soliciting, and it is remiss of your mother not to point this out to you." She then nodded into the stunned faces of the Blake women before turning to her brother. "Mathew, I need you to accompany me now, if you please. There is a matter I wish to discuss with Lord Kelkirk, and I think it will be of interest to you."

Claire felt her brother's eyes rest briefly on her face as she finished speaking, and then he bowed to the Blake ladies.

"Excuse me, ladies. My sister needs me."

They walked in silence through the throng until the Blake women were out of sight. Only then did Claire stop.

"Thank you."

She didn't pretend not to understand what Mathew was thanking her for.

"I have no wish to share a dinner table with that woman ever in my life. Therefore what I did was as much for my benefit as yours. Good evening, my lord," she then added. Turning her back on him, she then walked away without a backward glance.

"BELMONT, come and join us. Major Brantley is giving a detailed and riveting accounting of his daughter's latest equestrian achievements."

Simon had noticed Claire's brother standing very still, watching his sister walk away from him. His stance upright, his fists clenched. Mathew Belmont looked angry as he followed Claire with his eyes, and Simon wondered what she had said to make him feel that way. When he had visited them only a few days ago, Claire and her brother had seemed comfortable with each other, so he was all the more intrigued as to what had produced that reaction in the man.

"Lord Kelkirk." Belmont gave him and the others in his small group an elegant bow.

The major started into another long and detailed monologue of his daughter's exploits, which involved a lot of gesturing and horse terms.

"If you smile and nod at intervals, he doesn't notice you're not listening," Simon whispered to Mathew. "I am almost looking forward to the music starting just to shut him up."

Lord Belmont blew out a short breath, then nodded. "He's certainly an old windbag, yet harmless enough, I'm sure."

"You actually have more reasons than he to brag, Belmont. Your sister is the superior rider." Simon watched Mathew look down at his hands before answering.

"Yes, she has an excellent seat."

His voice held no inflection. Simon didn't know him that well, but he knew when a man was in the grip of some deep emotion. Belmont was displaying all the signs and trying not to show it, especially as he had failed to meet Simon's eyes.

"I can't imagine she can have been easy to control growing up. She has definitely held me to task a time or two," Simon said, deciding to prod him a bit for a response.

Mathew looked at him then, and Simon saw that mixed with the anger was sadness. His eyes were green, unlike his sister's, yet in the face, he saw Claire. They shared high cheekbones and long lashes, and perhaps there was something around the mouth.

"To my lasting regret, I did not have much to do with my sister growing up, Lord Kelkirk."

"I believe there is quite an age gap."

"Six years."

The silence that stretched between them then was not uncomfortable, as Belmont was lost in his thoughts and seemingly oblivious to his surroundings.

"We are being called to our seats, Belmont," Simon said finally, gently drawing the man back to the present.

"Of course. Please excuse me."

What the hell had that been about? he wondered as Mathew Belmont walked away without another word. The unease he had felt since finding Claire in that lane intensified. Something was very wrong in the Belmont household. He just needed to find out what.

"Kelkirk, my daughter has often expressed her interest in your seat and hands, says they are some of the finest in London."

Looking at Major Brantley, Simon swallowed his smile. He could take that statement in many ways, yet knew that the man was not deliberately lacing his words with innuendo. However he also knew that Brantley was looking for a husband for his daughter, and whilst Simon was not averse to the married state, he was averse to a woman who judged her men by the length of their hocks and strength of their seat.

"Well, lovely speaking with you, Major, and please give my regards to your charming daughter, but I must away, as the music is due to start."

He found Claire, but the seats to her left and right were taken, so he sat in the one behind. "Good evening, Miss Belmont."

She did not turn but did stiffen as he spoke. "Good evening, Lord Kelkirk."

"I understand we are to have Mozart this evening?"

"I believe so, yes."

"Tis most exciting, Lord Kelkirk," said the woman to Claire's right. "I believe Miss Fobersure is to be accompanied by Lady Lawn."

"Well, if that is indeed the case, I should imagine we are in for a night of unequalled excitement, Miss James."

He wasn't entirely sure, but thought that Claire may have snorted at his words.

"I was sincere in my praise, I assure you, Miss Belmont," he whispered in her ear. She shivered as his breath touched her neck. He had no further chance to talk, as the music began. His hopes when he had decided to come tonight were that the musicians were at least proficient, but he realized as Petunia Fobersure and Lady Lawn took the stage, he had made a grave error in attending. He had come to see Claire, of course, but even that thought did not help as the torture began. Simon watched Claire's fingers creep to her ears, which made him feel marginally better.

"Tut-tut, Miss Belmont," he said, once again leaning forward. One long strawberry blonde curl rested on her shoulder, and he wanted to lift it and roll it between his fingers to test the texture, instead he inhaled, and his head was filled with her scent. Subtle enough not to be overpowering, but disturbing none the less. He quickly sat back as his body responded. What was the matter with him? He'd never reacted like this to her before. He'd been aware of her yes, but never aroused. Focusing on the stage, his ardor soon cooled.

The music went on for what seemed like a day and a night until finally it ended, and the guests rose on a collective sigh of relief.

"We will now have dancing," Lady Waverly said with a beaming smile, unaware all her guests had a loud ringing in their ears, and most had vowed, silently, not to attend her musical evenings ever again.

Before he could stop her, Claire hurried away, following the other guests to where the dancing would begin. The woman was bloody elusive, he'd give her that. Pausing to secure a much needed glass of champagne, he then chatted briefly with a few friends before making his way through the crowd to the edge of the dance floor. Claire was dancing and appeared happy enough, smiling and chatting with her partner, although he could not read the expression in her eyes. The man she danced with was all but falling into her cleavage. He'd never seen her wear anything like that before. She always dressed with style and elegance. Often showing just enough soft pink skin to tantalize. Very rarely did she look like a bloody siren. Sensual and alluring, yes, however tonight Simon could feel his body growing tense just looking at her. He suddenly wanted to run one finger under his collar like a young whelp, as it felt tight against his throat. The color of the dress made her skin glow, and he had known she had lovely breasts but not quite how lovely. They would make any man's fingers twitch, showcased as they were in apricot satin this evening. Simon wasn't sure why he was angry about her dress or that other men were looking at her breasts, yet he was. So much so that when the dance stopped, he moved to intercept her. "My dance, I believe, Miss Belmont."

"I'm sorry, my lord, but I am promised to Lord Calvary."

"He's taken ill," Simon said, placing a hand on her spine and propelling her forward.

"You're lying. He was perfectly well not ten minutes ago." She tried to look over her shoulder to see if Lord Calvary was about, but Simon turned her in his arms as the waltz started, and they were soon moving together with the music.

"Miss Belmont, I never lie. Mr. Calvary is suffering from digestion issues. It seems his coat and breeches are too tight and restricting the airways." Simon looked down at her and tried to keep his eyes on her face instead of the lush swells above the bodice of her dress.

She didn't smile as he'd intended her to; in fact, the expression in her brown eyes was the same as her brother's had been earlier. He saw sadness, and exhaustion in every line of her pretty face.

"Yes, you do lie regularly, especially if it is to strengthen your claim."

"You wound me," he said, pulling her closer as they navigated their way around several couples. He had not danced often with Claire, usually because she was never short of partners and avoided Simon whenever she could. "How is your headache?"

"What headache?"

"The one you told Eva you had, when you sent a note around to her house explaining you would not be attending the Miller ball two nights ago." Interesting, she had lied to her best friend, but why? All this intrigue was making his head hurt.

"Oh yes, that headache. Much better, thank you, my lord." She avoided his eyes, by looking over his shoulder.

"I understand you are going with Daniel and Eva to Stratton tomorrow."

She nodded, still not looking at him.

"I was just talking with your brother, Claire. He appeared worried about something. Do you know what it is?"

Simon caught her as she tripped on his foot. He held her briefly before standing her back on her feet. Leaning forward so his mouth was against her ear, he then whispered, "What the hell is going on with you?"

Instead of censuring him for using coarse language in her presence, she simply pulled herself out of his arms.

"Thank you for the dance, Lord Kelkirk, but I fear my headache has returned. Thus I will find my mother at once and leave."

"Claire, I want to help you, please. Tell me what is wrong."

She tried to evade him as he reached for her arm, but

with so many prying eyes upon them, she could not, so he simply grabbed her hand and rested it on his sleeve.

"There is nothing wrong with me, my lord, other than a headache. Please take me to my mother at once."

"And your brother? Why did he look so sad when you walked away from him?"

Simon wasn't sure, as the room was filled with noise, but he thought she made a sound. However when he looked down at her, she had her usual calm smile in place. She wasn't calm, though. Her fingers dug into his arm through the sleeve of his jacket.

"My brother has much on his mind, my lord. I cannot furnish you with the reasons for his mood."

He wasn't going to get anything else out of her this evening, but he would tomorrow. He would make sure to get to Daniel's house before they left and see Claire then, and make her talk to him.

When they located Lady Belmont, the woman would not look at her daughter. Instead, she offered Simon a tight smile that resembled her children's. Whatever this was, it clearly involved the entire Belmont family.

"Excuse me. I shall find Lord Belmont now, Lady Belmont, as your daughter has a headache and wishes to leave at once." The older lady gave him a curt nod but still did not make a move toward her daughter.

Mathew Belmont was standing, looking out the window into the darkness. In one hand, he held a glass of champagne, which appeared untouched.

"Belmont, your sister is unwell and wishes to return home at once."

"Where is she?" His skin paled instantly, his eyes searching for Claire.

"I will take you to her."

They quickly made their way back through the throng to

Claire and Lady Belmont. Claire was standing silently beside her mother. Her hands were clenched, and she looked uncomfortable. Her mother looked much the same. Anyone watching them would have thought they were strangers, as they neither touched nor conversed.

"Are you unwell, Claire?"

Simon stayed back as Mathew reached for his sister. She stepped away from the hand Belmont was holding out, and it fell to his side.

"I wish to go home please, my lord, at once."

Not brother or Mathew but my lord. Claire's words sounded cold and detached.

"Of course we shall leave at once," Mathew said.

Simon then watched as Claire reluctantly took one of her brother's arms and Lady Belmont the other, and soon they had disappeared from his sight.

Simon could not rid himself of the feeling that in the three days since he'd visited the Belmont family, something very bad had happened, and although he had no right to pry into what that something was, he wanted to know. All of them were tense and unhappy, and the look in Claire's eyes would stay with him for the rest of the evening. Thirty minutes later, he realized he did not want to stay at the musical any longer, either. He would have an early night and be on Daniel's doorstep when Claire arrived. He would then question her, and this time she would bloody well answer him.

CHAPTER SEVEN

Claire waited until the house was quiet before sneaking into her brother's study. She placed her lamp on top of his desk, opened the drawer, and found the note. She then copied it word for word before replacing the original and folding her copy and slipping it into her dressing gown pocket. She then looked through the other drawers until she found a pouch of money. It was wrong to steal, especially from her brother, but he had left her with no other choice. Hurrying out into the hallway, she then made her way back to her room. She had walked these halls at night on her own before, however tonight she had a mission, and the fear of exposure was making her nervous. Only when she was safely inside her room with the door locked did she exhale loudly.

When she had realized her brother had no intention of going to rescue Anthony's child, she'd made plans to do so herself. Unfolding the note she had just copied, Claire re-read it, making sure it was clear and concise, as it would be the only aid she had in locating her niece or nephew.

I saw what happened to you in Tuttle Lane, Miss Belmont.

Therefore I have decided to give you one more chance, however this time you will have to go to Liverpool to retrieve your brother's possessions. Anthony Belmont's battalion passed through my family's village, and when they left, my sister was carrying his child. She has now passed away, but before her death, she told us who the father was and that she was to contact you, should she need help. My brother and I will wait for seven days at the Anchor tavern every day for an hour from midday. If you do not come, then we will have no choice but to abandon the child, as our ship will leave the following day. I have proof it is of your blood.

She had to go or live with the guilt for the rest of her life. She had pleaded with both her mother and Mathew, both had refused to yield, and now it was up to her to do something. She did not care if the child was French or English or any other nationality. It was Anthony's, therefore she would care for it as her own.

Tomorrow she was supposed to accompany Eva, Daniel and Georgia to Stratton at ten o'clock, and this had given her the opportunity she needed. In the morning, Claire would send a note to the duchess explaining she was sick and could not accompany her. She would pack her things and make her way to their house at eleven o'clock. She would then send her brother's carriage home and hire a carriage to take her to Liverpool. Failing this, because she had never hired a carriage, nor knew where to go to do so, she would catch the stagecoach. Mathew would think she was at Stratton, as he did not believe Claire would defy him.

Of course, so many things could go wrong with her planning. Eva and Daniel could decide to leave later, for instance, or someone could see her departing London. Yet she had to try. She couldn't discuss things with anyone, so she had to manage the journey herself, and the thought was terrifying. However, she was an intelligent woman. If her wits did not help, then she had the money she had saved, plus the full purse she'd stolen from her brother to bribe people. Dear lord, she hoped Mathew didn't blame the staff for the missing money. Claire dismissed this thought; she would deal with that upon her return if it needed to be dealt with.

She would be a young lady traveling alone, as she dared not take her maid because she was a terrible gossip. Claire had told her she would be using Eva's maid for the duration of her visit at Stratton. The journey to Liverpool would take three days, possibly four, and she would pretend to be a companion on her way to a new position, so as not to create too much attention. Claire could not allow herself to waver, because then she would think of the mammoth task before her, and the doubts would overcome her.

The night was long, and she worked and re-worked her plans, allowing for eventualities that may occur, until they were organized in her head. She pictured the child and wondered about the mother. The woman that she hoped had meant something to her brother. Would it have Anthony's eyes or even hers?

Eventually exhausted, she dozed, and it was her maid who woke her a few hours later. "Would you like a bath, Miss Belmont?"

Who knew when she would have another? "Yes, please, Janet."

She ate again in her room and then directed Janet to have her luggage taken down to the carriage. She dressed in peppermint, the color she had been told made her eyes seem almost green instead of the muddy hazel they actually were, and pulled on a darker pelisse. Tying the ribbons on her straw bonnet, she then studied herself in the mirror. This was a favorite hat of Claire's, and looking at the mirror, she hoped the façade she presented was exactly as it should be, a woman about to embark on a jaunt to the country with her dearest friend. Pinching her cheeks, she tried to put some color in them.

"You may leave now also, Janet, to visit with your family, and I will expect your return one week from today."

"Oh thank you, Miss Belmont."

Drawing in a deep breath, Claire then left her room. This would need to be the best acting performance of her life if she was to carry it off.

She tapped on the parlor door minutes later and opened it to find her brother and mother seated in silence. Mathew's eyes were wary as he looked at her. Lady Belmont appeared pale, but managed a small smile as Claire entered the room.

"I am leaving to accompany the duke and duchess to Stratton. I bid you good-bye, and I have no idea when I will return."

"Claire, you should eat something."

"Thank you, but I have no appetite, mother."

"Please, daughter, do not leave like this—"

"It is all right, mother. I am resigned, and wish to say nothing more on the matter. Now if you will please excuse me, I must not keep Eva and Daniel waiting." It hurt to turn away from them, even knowing they did not want the child. They were her family. Her mother, especially, had been a constant companion in her life since Anthony's death. She was about to defy them with her actions, and in doing so, change the direction her life would take entirely, from the one she now led. Especially as there would be a child in it.

"We are only—"

"Goodby." She cut off Mathew's words and hurried from the room, not wanting to stay a second longer. Instead, she walked back out the door before they could see her distress. She closed it firmly behind her, praying silently that it did not open again.

Her feet felt leaden and her heart heavy as she walked

down the stairs, her steps faltering when she saw Plimley at the base. If anyone would know she was lying, it was him, so she settled on a version of the truth. "Plimley, I am leaving for the Duke and Duchess of Stratton's house now."

He looked at her steadily as she continued down the staircase. "And is Janet to accompany you, Miss Belmont?"

"She is not. I have given her time off to spend with her family. She will return when I do."

Again, a steady look as she stopped before him on the last step. "I would ask that you send word if at any time you need assistance, Miss Belmont."

It was silly to want to cry because her brother's butler was there for her when her family was not. "I…I shall be all right, Plimley, and the country air will be wonderful, and just what I need."

"And I will reiterate that should you find yourself in any situation that you are not comfortable with, then you need only to send word, and I shall come."

"Th-thank you, but the duke and duchess will care for me, Plimley."

He didn't speak again, simply helped her down the stairs and through the door. He then opened the carriage and settled her inside. "Good-bye, Miss Belmont."

She wanted to urge Plimley inside with her, make him accompany her to Liverpool, but she could not, as he would think her reckless and alert Mathew.

"Good-bye, Plimley."

She didn't look back as the carriage made its way out onto the street. The skies were still grey, although the rain had stopped, and her journey to the Stratton residence took a mere ten minutes, as the hour was early and the traffic light. By the time her brother's carriage pulled into the driveway, she was beyond nervous. Claire had managed to leave her house without raising anyone's suspicions, now she had to get Toddy, her brother's driver, to drop her off and leave before he was aware that the duke and duchess were not in residence.

"Thank you, Toddy," Claire said in a brisk manner as the driver opened the door and handed her down. "You may leave after you've placed my bags on the front step. I shall simply tell the duchess I am here, as we are to leave directly."

"I can't see the carriage," the driver said, looking around the spacious driveway.

"It will be here in a few minutes, Toddy. Now please, just leave my bags there," Claire said, pointing to a space beside the steps.

"I'll knock on the door for you, Miss Belmont. Not right for you to be standing out here alone."

This was what came of having servants who'd known you since you were a child. They tended to forget you had grown up.

"There really is no need, Toddy—" The rest of Claire's words died in her throat as she heard the front door open.

Dear god, I am doomed.

"Wernham, you are a prince among men."

Why did it have to him, of all people, who was about to step outside after, apparently saying good-bye to the Stratton butler?

"The house will be quiet without—Claire?"

"Lord Kelkirk, how wonderful to see you. Are you to accompany us also? What a merry little party we shall be." Claire made herself smile as she hurried up the steps to the top, where Simon stood. Had she not been terrified, the confused look on his face would have made her laugh.

"Ah, Claire, they have already—"

She dug her fingers into his arm and squeezed, which made him wince. Claire needed to shut him up quickly before he alerted Toddy to the fact that the duke and duchess had already departed for Stratton. Standing on her toes, she brushed a kiss on his cheek and whispered the words. "Please, I'm begging you, just follow my lead."

He looked from her down to the driver who waited at the base of the stairs, and then nodded.

"Yes, a very merry party, Miss Belmont." His voice was flat and serious, and his eyes focused on her.

"That will be all now, Toddy, as you can see I am no longer alone," she said, dragging her eyes from Simon's to address the driver. Toddy gave her a bow, and in seconds, was in the seat and driving the carriage away.

"May I be of assistance, Lord Kelkirk, Miss Belmont?"

"Not at this moment, Wernham, thank you," Simon said. "If you will just give us a few minutes of privacy, I shall let you know if you are needed."

The butler closed the door quietly, and Claire now stood on the doorstep alone with Simon.

"You're pale, Claire. Why?"

She stiffen as he brushed the pad of his thumb beneath her eyes. Unlike her, he liked to touch and be touched—put a hand on a friend's shoulder or place a kiss on a cheek. Simon Kelkirk liked people to know he cared about them. Claire didn't want his touch because she needed to stay in control, and his kindness to her would prevent that from happening. In fact her nerves were strung so tight, she feared it would not take much for her to break.

Taking a step back, she said, "There is nothing amiss, my lord. I simply wish to take another journey. Now if you will excuse me, I must be on my way." Holding her breath, she then walked calmly back down the stairs, before exhaling. She then, picked up her bags, and started toward the gates. Claire had been fooling herself by thinking she would reach them.

"You think I will just let you walk away from me with

your luggage, alone, without either a carriage or servants?"

"Yes," Claire said, trying to shake off the hand he now had wrapped around her arm. "You are neither my husband nor brother. Therefore you have no say in what I do, so please release me, Lord Kelkirk."

They were still partially hidden from the road, but Claire knew that if someone moved close to the fence, they would be seen, so it was imperative she made her escape soon, and hire a hackney before someone recognized her.

"If you do not give me some answers soon, Claire, I will pick you and your luggage up and carry you into my carriage and drive around until you talk to me."

Stay calm, Claire. If she did, there was a chance she could walk away from here without him. But if she panicked he would not allow that. "I would ask that you simply turn your back and let me walk away, my lord. Will you do that? Because I must leave for somewhere at once, as there is not a moment to lose." Claire's heart thumped so loudly in her chest she was sure he must hear it.

"No, Claire, I cannot do that."

She could not outrun him, and there was no way she could manipulate him, as he was too clever for that. So what was she to do? She knew he was fair minded. Yes, they always appeared to be at odds with each other, and in truth, that was mostly her fault, but no one was closer to Eva and Daniel than he, and surely that was testament enough to his character. She had precious minutes to make a decision before someone saw both of them and her bags, so, taking a deep breath, she said what she had to. "I-I need to do something, alone. It will harm no one. I will return to London soon in perfect health, my lord."

"No." He said nothing further, just the one word, yet she heard the strength behind it, and knew her quest to leave London was slipping from her grasp.

Claire rarely stuttered when she spoke, nor did she ever physically reach for another person in support, yet now she did both. Dropping her bags, she reached out to him with one hand. "P-please, Simon, I must do this …th-thing. I'm begging you to walk away."

He caught her hand and placed her palm flat on his chest. She felt him through her gloves—the solid planes of his chest and the steady thud of his heart. A yearning grew inside her. The need to close the distance and rest her cheek on that broad chest was almost overwhelming.

"And where will this thing take you?"

She considered lying, but this man would not be easy to fool, so she decided on the truth. "To Liverpool. I-I need to get there, my lord, as soon as I can. The matter is extremely urgent, and no one can know I am going—not even my family. Please let me leave. I must, as there is so much at stake."

Simon could feel the tension running through Claire's body. The hand beneath his trembled, so he pressed it harder into his chest. What the hell was going on, and why was she here on Daniel's doorstep when he and his family had left for Stratton thirty minutes earlier?

"Claire, you have no driver. Therefore, I surmise you are to take this journey on a stagecoach or in a hired carriage. You also have no maid, which is not only dangerous but foolhardy for a gently bred woman with little experience of how life outside her world works."

"I must go, Simon." Her words were a plea. "Please, I am to harm no one or…or undertake anything illegal."

He snorted. "I know enough about you to know that, Claire, but I still cannot let you go alone."

"Oh, but I must—"

"However if you need to go, then I shall take you."

That surprised her. Her mouth opened and closed. She dropped her eyes to his chest and then lifted them again.

"No. I just need a carriage, and then I can get there myself."

"I will not let you travel alone to Liverpool, Claire. So you let me take you there, or I take you back to your brother."

He was standing so close to her, he could see the little flecks of green in her eyes, and the dark smudges beneath. She was exhausted.

"You would do that? Take me back to my brother if I do not let you accompany me?"

"I would, and not because you believe me capable of nefarious deeds, but because you are exhausted and vulnerable, and obviously about to do something that involves secrecy and evasion but more importantly, is forcing you to lie to your family."

"I must—"

"I am your friend, Claire," he interrupted her again. "I want to help you, and helping you is not sending you off to Liverpool in a carriage alone."

She bit her bottom lip, which drew his eyes to her mouth. He'd often wondered what she would taste like. Sharp and tart or sweet and alluring.

"I-I…"

"Claire, will you let me help you… please? It is obvious to me that you need someone to support you at the moment, and I know you well enough to realize that if I returned you to your brother, you would just find another way to do whatever it is you are doing. I know there is something going on with your family, a fool could see how you all were last night."

Her lashes fluttered closed briefly, almost as if the effort to keep them open was beyond her.

"I'm afraid to involve you in this, my lord, as I fear it may go badly."

"Are you sick?"

Her brow wrinkled as she looked up at him. "Sick? No, why would you ask that?"

"You were upset and scared when you ran into me in that lane, Claire. I thought of many reasons for you to be there, and that was one of them."

"Will you believe me when I tell you I am not sick?"

He searched her eyes and saw the truth, and the feeling of relief almost made him lightheaded. "I believe you. However if you are not ill, then you went there to meet someone."

He saw his words confirmed in her eyes.

"Let me go, Simon, please." The whispered words were a desperate plea he steeled himself to ignore.

"Sorry, but I can't let that happen." Taking the hand off his chest, he picked up her luggage and led her back to the house.

"Wernham," he said loudly, knowing the man was on the other side of the door. "I have changed my mind," he added as it opened and the butler reappeared. "Will you please rouse my driver from your kitchen, where he is indulging himself with cake, and have him bring my carriage around at once. I no longer wish to walk and will be escorting Miss Belmont home, as she has missed the duke and duchess's departure."

"At once, my lord."

"Simon, please."

He wasn't sure what she was trying to say, as she did not complete the sentence, but her eyes begged him to understand.

"Claire. I give you my word that you will get to Liverpool as soon as possible. However, I will need to know why, and that I am not placing you in danger before I do so. Firstly, however, I must notify—"

She grabbed the lapel of his jacket with her free hand. "Don't tell, Mathew, please. He thinks I am with Eva and Daniel."

"Have a little faith in me, woman." His voice was gruff. "I don't like deceiving your brother, but for you, I will do so, or at least until I know what this is about."

She didn't speak again, and their ride arrived minutes later. He quickly helped load her luggage and then urged her inside. Following, he shut the door behind them and pulled the curtains closed. "I do not want anyone to see you alone with me when you are meant to be with Daniel and Eva."

She nodded.

"I must stop at my house and collect a few things, Claire, and change carriages."

She nodded again but remained silent, and he wondered if she was too scared to speak or too tired. *What the hell is going on?* Fear and anxiety were written in every line of her body. She was coiled so tightly, Simon wondered if she would shatter if he touched her. He'd believed her when she'd said she wasn't sick, yet whatever this was about was serious enough to make the indomitable Miss Belmont vulnerable.

He remained silent as they journeyed through the streets of London but kept his eyes on her, while hers remained on the hands that were clenched in her lap. She looked the elegant society lady she always did. Her dress was soft and hugged her lovely body, and her bonnet framed her face, yet if one looked close enough, they would see the desperation.

His house was close, and they were soon pulling up outside. Moving to the edge of the seat, he took her hands, forcing her to look at him. "I want your word that you will sit here and await my return, Claire."

"I promise."

"If you run, I will follow, and you will not be pleased to see me when I catch you."

"I have promised, my lord," she snapped, making him smile. It was good to see a glimpse of the woman he knew so well. On impulse, he kissed her cheek and then left the carriage.

He ordered Merlin to have his traveling coach brought around and to be ready to drive him to Liverpool. Ben would sit beside him, and both would be armed. Simon wasn't sure why he wanted his two best coachmen with him. Perhaps because Claire was to be inside. He ordered it to be loaded with food and blankets. After telling his staff he was leaving for a few days, he then broke his valet's heart, telling him he would not be required for the journey.

"But your neckties!"

"I can tie a bloody knot, Sully. I am not a complete imbecile." Simon pulled some papers and money out of the locked drawer in his desk, then tucked a pistol into the top of his boots.

"But your boots, my lord—who will clean them?"

"No one, and all who see me will wonder at the capabilities of my valet," Simon said, trying to think what else he would need. The problem was he didn't know what was a foot. Therefore he had no idea what to expect or, indeed, what to prepare himself for.

His valet whimpered as Simon grabbed the neckties off him and stuffed them into the case. "You have no brush," Sullivan said, scampering across the room to grab one.

Taking it, Simon hurled it into the bag beside the neckties. "Now be quiet and fasten that bag. I must leave at once."

Sullivan muttered of dire circumstance such as missing buttons and dirty cuffs all the way to his front door, which Simon opened and closed firmly in his face.

Claire had not moved and did not utter a word as he opened the door and held out his hand.

"Come, we need to change coaches for the journey."

They traveled in silence until London was well behind them. He'd thought to give her time to get her thoughts together and feel comfortable in the carriage with just him for company. Hell, he needed the time to think about the change in his circumstances. This morning, his most pressing worry had been whom he would fence with, now Daniel was away. Looking across the carriage, he wondered again what this was all about. Claire wasn't the sort to take risks or break rules. He'd never seen her do anything even remotely scandalous until that day in the lane when she'd lifted her skirts and fled from him. Sensing his eyes were on her, she looked up.

"You will have to tell me soon, Claire, as I will not leave you alone until we return to London. I will be present when you reach Liverpool and be with you as you do whatever it is that you intend to do. In fact, you will probably come to think of me as your shadow until I have you safely returned to the bosom of your family."

"I doubt I will ever again be comfortable around my family, my lord." He watched as she slowly unclenched her fingers after speaking these ominous words, and then, pushing the curtain aside, she looked through the windows. "Do you think we could open them now?"

He did as she requested and then sat back and waited. She fiddled with her gloves, smoothed her skirts, and finally, she took off her bonnet and placed it on the seat beside her. He knew she wasn't deliberately trying to delay telling him. She was simply gathering her words.

"I would firstly like to thank you, my lord, for taking me in your carriage when you had no idea what I was undertaking or why. I fear few people would be so generous."

"Do you know, Claire, I believe that is the first compliment you have ever paid me." That produced a small smile, but she did not comment. Instead, she began her story.

"I do not need to ask that you keep what I tell you a secret, because soon you'll understand the gravity of the situation." She didn't speak in the confident, haughty tone she saved especially for him. Her words were husky, almost as if her throat was raw. "The day before I ran into you, my lord, in that lane, I had received a note telling me my brother Anthony—he's—"

"I know about Anthony, Claire."

She nodded. "The note stated that Anthony had left something in France and I was to go to Tuttle Lane and meet someone there to collect it."

"However you ran into me, and that put an end to that."

She nodded again before continuing. "Do you remember the day you and Eva brought Georgia to visit with me?"

This time, Simon nodded.

"My brother intercepted a note meant for me whilst you were there, and that is why he did not rejoin us."

Simon said nothing as she fell silent again, her fingers were now pleating the skirts of her dress. He was good with silence. He'd had plenty of practice in his youth, and he had soon realized it made people uncomfortable—so uncomfortable, often they uttered the first things that came into their heads, which in some cases, were the last things they wanted anyone to hear.

"The note said I was to be given another chance, and that Anthony had a child and I was to go to Liverpool to collect it, and if I did not go within the time they stipulated, then it would be abandoned. I have to call it… it, as I have no idea whether I have a niece or nephew." These last words tumbled out in a breathless rush and they left Simon sitting in stunned silence.

CHAPTER EIGHT

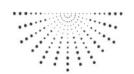

A myriad of scenarios had run through Simon's head since he had found her on the steps of Daniel's house, yet none of them had come close to this. He'd had her fleeing from a man her brother had wanted her to marry, or alternatively, fleeing to a man her brother disapproved of. Neither of these had sat well with him.

"And you are going to get the child?" Simon questioned her.

"Yes, because my mother and Mathew will not." She lifted her chin, and he saw the determination. She would go to Liverpool even if she had to walk all the way.

"And you went to that lane to see these people who have the child, just as you are now going to Liverpool on your own, with no support, and presumably a vast amount of money tucked away on your person?" Simon hadn't meant to raise his voice, but he couldn't believe anyone would attempt anything so foolish alone.

"I had no other choice, can't you see? I will not let my niece or nephew be abandoned on the streets of Liverpool. If need be, I will take him or her and disappear to one of my brother's estates. However I will do this for Anthony, as he would have done for Mathew, were their roles reversed."

"You were going to travel by stagecoach or hired carriage for a three-day journey to Liverpool," Simon continued, undaunted by the fact she was upset. Bloody little fool—anything could have happened to her even before she'd left London if he hadn't intercepted her. "You were to stay with the other travelers dressed like that?" He pointed to her clothing. "Christ, Claire, I had thought you a woman of sense. It appears I was wrong."

She leaned toward him, her eyes shooting sparks. "Don't insult me, my lord. I have an old cloak and bonnet to change my appearance. Furthermore," she added as he scoffed loudly, "I am doing what the circumstances necessitated I do. Should I perhaps have asked my brother's coachman to drive me, or perchance the butler to book me a ticket on the stage to Liverpool?"

"I expected you to exercise intelligence!"

"You know very well were I to tell any of my brother's staff, they would have passed that information on to him. I could not allow that to happen."

Simon tamped down his anger. "I do not know Mathew well, Claire, yet he does not seem an unreasonable man. I'm sure he felt he was making the right decisions for his family. Did you try to talk this through with him? What of your mother? She would want to know if Anthony's child was alive, surely."

Pain flashed across her face. "My mother does what my brother tells her to, and as he does not believe there is a child, Lord Kelkirk, neither of them will take steps toward checking the validity of the claim. Mathew refuses to see reason. Therefore, he has forced me to take action.

Simon wasn't quite so sure that Mathew Belmont's actions were unreasonable, in fact, he thought the man was reacting to what he believed was a threat to his family. He was protecting his sister from harm, and ensuring his mother's heart was not broken again. Simon could not say his reactions would have been any different, were he in the man's shoes.

"I'm sure given time, Mathew—"

"There is no time, Lord Kelkirk. As I have explained, we must arrive at the port of Liverpool three days hence at the latest." Her hands fluttered and then settled on her lap as she spoke. "If you have no wish to help me now you know, then drop me where the stage passes through, and I shall secure a ticket."

He looked at her for several seconds. "I will ignore that ridiculous statement and instead tell you to calm down, Claire, as we are simply talking through this situation, and you are distressed enough already."

Normally, she would have told him exactly what she thought of his words, demanded he retract those ridiculous statements, yet she did not. Instead, she closed her eyes on a tired sigh.

"I must go, Simon, or I shall live my life wondering if I have abandoned my brother's child."

"We will go to Liverpool, Claire, but right at this moment, you look as if you need some sleep. Close your eyes. We have many hours of travel ahead of us, and you will need your strength for what is about to come, I'm sure."

"If only I could."

"If only you could what? Sleep?" Simon frowned at her words.

"We are to spend nights on the road, my lord. How will we explain my lack of companion?" She ignored his question in favor of asking her own.

"Now you are worried about propriety?"

"If I was on my own, I would simply say I was a

companion traveling to my next position. I am not without wits, after all, and am sure I could have fooled anyone I met."

His eyes ran over her briefly. "You look like no governess I have ever met."

"And of course you are acquainted with several, seeing as you have children, my lord."

Simon smiled at her tart return. "As to your question, tonight we will spend at a small cottage a friend of mine owns. I know where the key is and there will be supplies on hand. We will worry about the next stop when it is before us."

All fight left her as he spoke. "I am putting you to a great deal of trouble, Lord Kelkirk, when in truth, I do not deserve to do so. I also know that my reputation will be in tatters, should anyone find out about this journey, yet that will not stop me from undertaking it, nor are you in any way responsible, should I be found out."

"A very pretty speech, Miss Belmont, and thank you for caring about my pristine reputation. However I'm a grown man, and the choices I make are mine alone."

"Please, Lord Kelkirk, I would not—"

"I think we can dispense with my title, and you can call me Simon all the time now, Claire, don't you?" He was gratified at her small smile. "Now tell me why I shouldn't trouble myself on your behalf?"

She did not hide behind lies. "Because I have not always treated you as well as I should, Simon."

He moved to take the seat next to her and lifted one of her hands. "To be fair, I have provoked that reaction from you."

"Not always and not to start with."

He searched her face. "Why did you feel the need to constantly provoke me?"

She didn't prevaricate or sweeten the words.

"I wish I knew."

She looked so small suddenly—small and sad—and he couldn't stand to see her hurting. "Will you let me help you, Claire? Just for a while, let me keep you safe?" Simon closed the distance between them and placed a gentle kiss on her lips. "Just this once, there is no need to show the world how strong you are, as I am the only one here to see."

"I can't, Simon, because I fear if I let go, then I will fall apart."

He wrapped an arm around her and pulled her into his side. She was tense, but did not fight him.

"Did you know Lord Henkle fell face first in the punch last night, Claire? It was quite a sight, especially when the punch splashed out of the bowl and covered Miss Dorothy Plummer's new satin slippers." She didn't answer him, so he continued to tell her tales of society until he felt her body soften against him. Resting his feet on the opposite seat, he shifted, turning slightly so she lay against his chest.

"Be still, Claire," he said as she protested. Surprisingly, she did as he asked, and then, with a tired sigh, she placed a hand on his heart and relaxed. He found a long strawberry blonde curl trailing down her back, picked it up, and rolled it around his fingers.

He had known Claire Belmont was a woman who had the ability to unsettle him, yet holding her like this, he realized he had underestimated his feelings for her. She smelt sweet and felt soft in his arms, but there was so much more to his attraction for her now. The feelings she stirred inside him should have had him dropping her at the nearest posting house and fleeing back to London. He wanted to protect her and make her smile again, and the feel of her pressed against him was a sweet form of torture.

"You're a good man, Simon."

"You sound disappointed by that observation."

"I'm disappointed I did not allow myself to see it before now," she corrected him.

"Sadly, I know when this is all over, you'll retract those words and once again be tart-mouthed toward me." Simon sighed, his breath stirring her hair. Her hand smoothed the front of his jacket, and even through the layers of cloth, he felt her touch.

"I shall try not to be."

He knew that at this moment in time, Claire had no defenses in place. If he pressed her, there was every chance she would tell him whatever he wanted. Yet he could not do that to her... or maybe he could, just a bit.

"But where will the fun be in that? Lord, don't tell me you will start simpering and giggling behind your hand when I draw near? It would shock me, Claire, to the soles of my large feet. I love to watch your eyes narrow as they turn on me. It is an honor that only I can make you drop that polite façade the rest of society sees."

"Most evenings I am simply hiding behind that façade of respectability, Simon."

"Are you not respectable then?" He lifted the curl and ran it down his cheek before speaking.

"Of course I'm respectable, but sometimes it is a struggle."

Her words made him smile as he imagined her suddenly doing something rash in a ballroom, like lifting her skirts and kicking her legs in the air.

"We all have other sides to us, Claire."

"Do you?"

He thought about his estate and the aunt and uncle who lived there and the large glasshouse that enclosed his treasures. Yes, he had secrets and other sides to him, too. Perhaps they were not dangerous or exciting. Nor was he ashamed of them. However, they were his secrets to hold close—his alone to share with whom he wanted, when he wanted to.

"Yes," he said softly. "I have another side to me that only a few people know about."

"You like to read those dreadful sensation novels my mother is so fond of, don't you?"

Simon snorted and gave the curl a tug. "I do not."

"You like to dress in purple satin and wear jewel heeled slippers away from the prying eyes of the public?" She'd always had the ability to make him smile, even when he'd wanted to shake her until her teeth rattled. "No. I leave the jewel heeled slippers to Captain Cummings."

"He is such a silly man and cannot seriously think he looks anything but foolish, can he, Simon?"

"To his mind, he is a man of elegance and beauty, a pinnacle for the rest of us to aspire to, and if he causes no one harm, Claire, then who are we to change him?"

She sighed, not a delicate lady's sigh but a gusty man's one. "Oh dear, not only are you a good man but a kind one, too."

"Poor Claire. Are your illusions being shattered?"

"I think I always knew you were a good man, Simon. After all, we share friends."

"Georgia loves me best, however—she told me."

Her laugh sounded rusty. "Will you tell me your secrets, Simon?"

"I think not. At least, not yet."

She was silent, and he could almost hear her thinking as she tried to guess what his secrets were.

"D-do you have a child, Simon?"

"Do I seem like the kind of man who would have a child or two hidden away?" Her answer suddenly meant a great deal to Simon.

She lifted her head to look at him, and he lost himself in her lovely eyes. "No, you do not, but then, neither did my brother," she said solemnly.

"God I'm sorry, Claire. I didn't think—"

She placed her gloved fingers over his mouth. "You have nothing to apologize for, and I should never have asked you that question, as you are indeed, an honorable man and would not abandon children to their fates."

The sadness in her eyes broke his heart.

"I should imagine Anthony never knew of his child, Claire, so do not judge him harshly without all the facts."

"Do you think so?"

Simon nodded.

"I hope you are right," she said and then muffled a yawn behind one hand.

"Rest now, Claire, as you will need your strength for what is to come." Pressing her head into his chest once more, he leaned his head back on the seat and closed his own eyes, and in minutes he slept.

Reluctantly, Claire pushed herself upright and away from the warmth and comfort of Simon's chest as she felt his body soften into slumber. Moving to the opposite seat, she looked at him. She had often studied people when they slept— mostly her mother whilst she caught naps between journeys —and tried to understand the miracle that had put them into the blissful yet elusive state called sleep. Claire had once been like that, able to sleep for long hours and awake refreshed, but no longer. Now she woke irritable and haggard. Such a small thing to many, yet to her it meant so much. Envy was a sin, and she had it tenfold whenever she saw someone sleeping peacefully.

She shouldn't have involved Simon in her problems, because now he was committed to helping her, and would stay at her side until she had completed her journey. He was a gentleman, she knew that, but also a good person. She had embroiled him in her troubles and for that she was sorry. He was loyal to her, but also Daniel and Eva. Would he tell them what she had done?

Claire studied him while he slumbered. His face relaxed in sleep, yet there was no doubting he was a handsome devil. That silver and black hair stood him apart from others, and according several woman of her acquaintance gave him a distinguished air. As usual he was immaculately dressed, and one large hand rested against the seat whilst the other sat on his thigh. His big feet were braced beside her. Splaying her fingers, she put them next to the hand closest. They were huge, dwarfing hers.

If anyone found them alone together, she would be ruined, and he would be the recipient of her family's anger. She would not allow that to happen. If she was ruined for rescuing her brother's child, then it was her ruin alone, not Simon's. He thrived as a highly sought-after bachelor in London society, and she would not be the one to bring about his downfall. If she had to leave London and retire quietly to the country, it would not destroy her as it would him.

Of course, now her chances of marriage were extremely unlikely. Few men would understand about the child, and add to that her sleep problems, and she did not present a very attractive prospect. In fact, Claire doubted she would find love and a man with such an understanding nature.

He would understand. Claire looked across the carriage at the slumbering man and ignored the little voice inside her head.

Leaning back in the seat, she let thoughts come and go as she watched Simon sleep. He didn't move. His hands didn't twitch or clench, and his head never rolled from side to side. It stayed perfectly still on the back of the seat. He didn't snore or snuffle. His breathing was steady and even. She watched him closely as the carriage rolled on for mile after mile. She watched and wondered what the child's name was as her mind filled with scenarios of what her future would now hold. Could she raise a child alone? What life would it have as a bastard? Whatever that life was to be, it would have her protection, Claire vowed.

It was as the carriage began to slow that he opened his eyes and looked straight at her. He gave her a slow, sleepy smile and then stretched like a large cat.

"I appear to have slept the journey away, madam. I do beg your pardon for being such a terrible traveling companion."

His voice was deep and husky from lack of use and ran like heated honey down her spine.

"Do you always sleep so deeply?" Claire questioned before she could stop herself.

"I believe so. Sleeping has always been one thing I truly excel at."

"How lucky you are." Claire kept her features calm as he gave her a searching look.

"Did you sleep?"

"Of course," she lied.

He slid forward on the seat, trapping her between his legs again, and then grabbed her chin as she tried to look away from him.

"Why did you not sleep?" he said, studying her face, "when you so obviously needed it?"

"I-I do not sleep well in carriages."

He was so close, she could see a small brown freckle just above his right eye. She'd never seen it before, and for some reason it made her stomach flutter.

"You also do not lie very well, Miss Belmont."

"I— what do you mean? I'm not lying."

"Of course you are, and you're atrocious at it, but the question of why you do not sleep can wait for another day.

Right now, I shall tell my driver to stop somewhere quiet so we may eat and stretch our legs.

Minutes later, the carriage stopped, and she was pleased to step down and stretch her legs. They were beside a narrow, winding stream that was flanked by plenty of soft grass and shaded trees.

"Should we not press on, Simon? I fear we won't reach our destination by nightfall."

"As you have no idea where that destination is, how do you know how far away it lies?"

Claire huffed out a breath.

"I have promised you we will reach our destination by the time you wish to. The rest, I'm afraid you will have to leave up to me and my coachmen, Merlin and Ben. Now," he added, reaching for the basket and blanket, "a few minutes to stretch our legs and fill our stomachs will not delay us overly."

She trailed behind him as his long legs carried them toward the stream, where he placed a blanket beneath the shady branches of a tree and a large basket beside it.

"Simon, when I have the child, will you let me find my own way back to London, please?" Claire had not meant to say the words so quickly, she had wanted to speak slowly, in a calm, rational manner. Standing nervously at the edge of the blanket, she looked down at him, now sprawled on most of it. So much had changed between them since this morning, and she wasn't sure how to cope with those changes.

"Be quiet and sit, Claire, for pity's sake. How am I to eat with you trying to ruin my digestion?"

"I can hardly believe any of this is happening, Simon, but most of all, I cannot believe I have coerced you into my mess. It was very wrong of me, and I want you to leave."

"What, now? Have you no heart, woman? I'm hungry, and it is grossly unfair of you to send me on my way in this state.

Plus, if I left you here alone, you would suffer an uncomfortable night on the cold ground." He was smiling as he teased her.

"This is not a laughing matter, Simon. I have no wish for you to suffer because of my problems."

He moved quickly. One of his hands caught hers, and he pulled her down toward him, catching her as she tumbled. He then sat her on the blanket as one would a doll. She tried to clench her fingers to stop him from removing her gloves, but soon he had them off. He then had handed her a piece of bread onto which he'd slapped a thick slice of ham.

"Eat."

"No one has ever handled me like that before," she said stunned, yet still sitting as he had placed her.

"Perhaps if they had, you would not be so contained."

"I'm not contained!"

Simon simply gave her a steady look before saying, "Eat," once more.

Claire ate because, strangely, she was hungry. For days she had nibbled at her meals, but now she suddenly found herself ravenous. As soon as she finished whatever he had thrust at her, he would hand her something else, and she continued to eat until she could not force down another morsel.

"I was hungry," she said, stating the obvious.

"So you were."

"Simon, we must talk."

"No, Claire, we mustn't. Now start folding the blanket so we can leave, as there is still some distance to cover before reaching our lodgings for the night."

Claire did as he asked and then followed him back to the carriage. Once there, he re-opened the hamper and gave his drivers some food, and soon, they were once again on their way. She would talk to him when they reached their lodgings. She would be calm and decisive. She would set out her case, and he would see reason and leave. Strangely, the thought of him leaving filled her with unease. Something about knowing Simon was with her made the entire journey and what she must do seem easier.

CHAPTER NINE

"Your coachman has an unusual name, Simon."

"Yes. Ben is an extremely unusual name."

"You know very well I mean Merlin."

"Ah, Merlin. Yes, an odd name for a difficult man, Claire, who, of late, has been something of a trial to me."

"What did he do?"

"My maid is with child, and it appears he is the father."

"Oh dear, that is quite a difficult situation. What will you do?" Her question was one of genuine concern. Simon was pleased that she cared for the plight of his servants... which was foolish, if he thought about it. Why did her opinion matter to him so much?

"What would you do?" He was curious to know if she would have done the same as he had.

"I would ask both if they wanted to marry each other, then help them to do so." She said the words instantly, taking no time to think, and as they echoed his own, he could find no fault in them.

"Merlin is to marry Jilly as soon as it can be arranged, as he has assured me he cares for her and her for him. I will also help to secure them a house to live in once they are married if they need my assistance."

Her look was one of surprise. She had obviously not thought he would handle the matter as he had. "Did you think I would throw her out of my house, Claire?"

She shook her head. "No, of course not. I knew you would be fair. However, I did not realize you would be so generous."

He gave her a steady look. "You do not have a very high opinion of noblemen, Miss Belmont—more specifically, me."

"I'm sorry. I did not mean to be disrespectful, Simon. Forgive me. I am just not myself."

"Perhaps you will be more yourself, Claire, if you close your eyes," he added after she tried to hide a large yawn behind one hand. "I will wake you if need be."

She did as he asked and leaned her head back on the seat. However she did not sleep; he could tell by her breathing and the way her body did not relax into slumber. Her hands, too, remained clenched in her lap. Tension was clear in every line of her body. He could not blame her, after all what she was about to do would change her life in many ways. Even if there was no child.

Simon watched her as he thought about the next few days. They would spend tonight alone in a house with no servants, and the days after that would be spent in accommodations used by many. He would need to protect her as best he could, and he hoped they encountered no one who knew them. Perhaps he should say they were related or married? If they were discovered, she would be ruined beyond repair. Her reputation would be blackened, and even her dearest friends, the duke and duchess, could do nothing to salvage it.

Night had fallen as finally the carriage rolled to a stop. He opened the door, stepped down onto the cobbled driveway, and held out his hand. Claire's fingers felt soft in his. Her gloves were tucked into his pocket, and he held them firm as he led her toward the house.

"It looks a lovely little cottage, Simon," she said looking at the façade before them.

"Yes, it has a charm of its own."

He led her to the front steps and told her to wait whilst he found the key, which was placed under a pot around the side of the house. Returning, he opened the door and then urged her inside.

"Where shall Merlin and Ben sleep?"

"In the stables, Claire. There is a comfortable loft that will suit them both. Now find some candles whilst I collect our luggage."

It did not take him long to organize his coach and horses and ensure his drivers were comfortable before carrying their bags into the cottage.

She was not where he'd left her. Dropping the luggage, he walked through the kitchen and found Claire in a small parlor. She had lit several candles and was walking around the shelves studying book titles.

"The owner is an avid gardener, Simon, if these books are any indication."

"He is."

"I sometimes wish I could live in a place like this." She sounded wistful as she turned slowly, taking in the pale walls and soft rugs scattered on the floor. It was a special place to Simon, the first home he had thought of as his own. This was where he ran when he needed solitude or a place to think. It was small, consisting of two rooms upstairs and three down. It was simple and decorated for comfort rather than style, and he loved every inch of it.

"You want to live in a house with five rooms?" He watched as she pressed her face to the small paned windows, which he knew led to a garden filled with the sweet scent of a hundred blooms and enough color to make even Miss Bugs happy.

"Sometimes I wish to escape, Simon, if only for a day."

"Why don't you?"

Her laugh held no humor. "How like a man with no restrictions to suggest such a thing." Moving back to the bookshelf, she skimmed her fingers slowly along the spines as she walked. "I cannot even leave my house alone to shop for a new bonnet without someone demanding to know where I have been and why. Were I to simply climb on my horse and leave London, my mother's heart would give out, and my brother would lock me in my room for days."

"I can see how that could be a deterrent," Simon said, moving to lean against the wall. "However I, too, have crosses to bear."

"Do tell, my lord, of these crosses you bear," she said, stopping to stare at him. The distance between them was not great, and he could see she was nervous being here alone with him. She was a young woman who had never done anything but follow the rules, and now she was breaking them in a spectacular fashion.

"I, as an eligible bachelor with healthy teeth and a full purse, am a hunted species." Ignoring her scoffing sounds, he continued. "I am tittered at, called upon to pick up gloves and handkerchiefs, and must listen while mothers extol their daughters' virtues until I want to gnash my teeth."

"Oh please, you cannot expect me to believe the adoration you receive nightly is not welcome."

She was beautiful in candlelight, the flicker casting her skin and hair golden. Somehow here in his home, she appeared approachable and imminently more touchable.

"From some it is welcome," he said slowly, "however, when Lady Pepper pretends to trip and land on me, it is not. That woman could flatten an entire cavalry of the King's

Dragoon Guards." Her smile was like a light appearing at the end of a tunnel. Seeing her unsettled and hurt today had affected him, but that brief flash of teeth made him feel lighter. "Besides, I had you most evenings to un-stroke my ego, Miss Belmont."

The smile fell from her lips.

"Claire, I'm joking with you. I enjoy our conversational battles."

"As do I, but again you have highlighted that I have no right to put you in the position I have, considering my treatment of you."

"And again I will state, that I am an adult and being with you is my choice."

"Thank you, Simon. That is most kind of you. Now where shall I sleep, as I would like to retire for the night, please?"

Pushing off the wall, he reached for her bags. "There are two rooms upstairs, both off the hallway. You shall take the one on the right. There is bedding in the hall cupboard."

Hesitating briefly, Simon watched her as she bobbed a little curtsey and then hurried off in the direction he had indicated. He collected her bags and followed.

The cupboard stood open, and she was inside pulling out several items when he reached her.

"Do you need help with your bed, Simon?"

"I can make my own bed, Claire, but thank you for the offer." Simon opened the door to her room and took her bags inside.

"Can you really?"

"Yes I can, really."

"I apologize if I sound skeptical, Simon. I just have never thought of you as a man who can do chores such as making a bed. I do not know many noblemen who could."

"I had wondered when she would make a reappearance,"

Simon said, watching as she pulled the cover back on her bed and started to make it.

"Who?"

"The woman who challenges me in London. I have seen very little of her today, and I'm glad she still lurks inside you."

"I am not being challenging, Simon. I was merely stating a fact."

"That you believe all noblemen cannot make beds," he said, admiring the shape of her bottom as she bent to tuck in the sheet.

"I do not deliberately challenge you."

"Never tell me you were born with that sharp tongue?"

The look she gave him was supposed to be fierce, yet it was merely pathetic when accompanied by a yawn.

"It is my duty toward your future wife not to pander to your considerable ego, Simon. Someone needs to set you back on your heels a time or two, and the task is not an onerous one, I assure you."

She made the bed as she did everything, quickly, efficiently, and perfectly.

"Can I help it if people like me?"

"Women like you," she clarified, smoothing one slender hand over the final blanket. "Women are foolish around you, Simon. All that fawning and simpering is aweful to watch. I have no idea how you countenance it."

Simon laughed as she frowned. "So it is your duty to ensure I do not have all seven deadly sins and that my future wife is presented with a malleable husband she can manipulate?

He saw the flash of another smile as she turned to pick up a pillow and place it on the bed. "I am far too tired to give this conversation my full attention. Therefore we shall discuss it further when I am once again capable of putting you in your place."

And with those words, the smile was gone again, and in its place was a frown that revealed she was thinking once more about what she must do.

"I shall take that reprieve, Miss Belmont, and collect us both water for washing and then bid you goodnight." Simon made himself walk out the door and close it softly behind him before he took her in his arms and held her until the fear had gone.

After collecting the water and giving her some, he entered his room and quickly made the bed. He then stripped to the waist and washed, the cool water feeling good after a day's travels. He pulled off his boots, opened the window, and lay on the bed in his breeches. His mind immediately went to Claire and what she had set out to do. He didn't know many women who would have undertaken such a task. He also didn't doubt there was every likelihood she would have succeeded without him, yet just thinking about her alone out there made him shudder. Closing his eyes, he hoped she was now in bed as he was, because she needed sleep desperately. Two minutes later, he was slumbering.

CLAIRE HAD WASHED and pulled on her nightdress. Unpinning her hair, she then remembered there was no way of getting it back on top of her head tomorrow. She should have left it up, as it was unlikely she would sleep tonight anyway. Brushing it vigorously, she thought she could perhaps manage a simple bun or even a plait. Lying on the bed, she looked into darkness and tried not to think about Simon doing the same just a few feet from her. Would he be asleep already, his big body slumbering peacefully until morning? Claire closed her eyes and tried to clear her thoughts.

Was the child a boy or a girl? How old was it? The questions suddenly began to roll around again inside her head.

Determined to get a few hours sleep, she fell back on what she did most nights. Counting the doors in her brother's townhouse and then the servants. The problem was that as soon as she lay down, she was suddenly wide awake, and usually stayed that way.

After several hours, Claire gave up and slipped out of bed and lit her candle. At least if she walked about or read, her thoughts were focused on something other than her problems. Wrapping a shawl around her, she went barefoot from her room. She tiptoed down the hall, hoping Simon would stay asleep. Remembering the carriage and how deeply he had slept, she thought it was likely he would. In fact, Claire was fairly certain it would take a herd of stampeding cows to disturb him. The bottom stair creaked, but she heard no sound from behind her, so she made her way back into the room that held all the books. There were so many of them. Lifting the candle, she ran her hand along the titles and settled on a work about how to nurture seedlings. Surely that would be boring enough to put her to sleep.

"Claire, what are you doing?"

She spun around so quickly that the book fell from her hands and the spine split as it landed on the hard floor. "You startled me, Simon!" Placing the candle on the table, Claire dropped to her knees and gathered the broken book into her hands carefully. "I will have it fixed. Your friend need not know."

Large, warm hands wrapped around hers as she stood. He took the book from her and then turned her to face him. "It's a book on gardening, Claire. I'm sure no one is going to be concerned if it is a bit damaged."

He wore no shirt, his chest bare, and Claire could feel the heat from it against her hands as he moved closer.

"I should have been more careful." She couldn't look at him. She was too tired, her emotions were in turmoil, and he was nearly naked. She had never seen a man's chest before.

"Why are you not asleep?"

"Because I don't."

"You don't sleep?"

"Must we have this conversation now? You should return to your bed and let me read up on how to nurture my seedlings."

"I'm sure your seedlings will be fine, Claire. Now tell me what you mean by, 'I don't sleep.'"

"It's really quite a simple concept to grasp. I don't sleep well," Claire snapped, and then she tried to step away from him, but he simply slipped his big arms around her and held her still.

"Let me go, please."

"Why don't you sleep well?" He ignored her request.

She dropped her head back and looked up at him. His hair stood on end, and his eyes were sleepy, and he looked dangerous and somehow more disturbing than he did when he was the immaculately attired gentleman she knew. His chest was broad and muscled, and if she just took a step forward, she could fall on it, as Lady Pepper had. Dear god, she needed to move away quickly. "Because I can't."

"How long have you not slept well for?"

"It feels like forever," Claire said, feeling her resistance flee as she thought of all those nights that had stretched long and lonely before her. "And I'm so tired, Simon."

"I know, sweetheart. I can see that you are."

"Don't… please."

"Don't please what?" His hand now cupped her cheek, and his thumb was rubbing the skin. Claire was sure an imprint would be there forever.

"Don't call me that. Don't be nice to me, because I am not quite myself tonight."

"You obviously have a very good reason to not be yourself, Claire. Will you let me help you go to sleep?"

She shook her head. "I have tried many things, Simon, and still I only snatch an hour or two during the night. Plimley has made many suggestions, but none of them have worked."

"Your brother's butler knows?"

Claire nodded again. "Plimley is not like a normal butler."

"He certainly doesn't look like one."

"He's always been there for me."

His thumb caressed her cheek again. "I'm glad he was there for you, Claire."

She heard the unspoken question in his voice. Simon wanted to know why her butler had been there for her, yet her family had not. She was relieved when he chose to ask her something else.

"When did this sleeplessness start?"

This was a pointless conversation to be having. After all, Simon could do nothing for her. He just needed to leave her alone with the book. Soon it would put her to sleep for a few hours so that in the morning she could cope. "I'm quite all right, Simon, really. This is what I'm used to, and I should let you go back to your bed."

"So you can walk the halls? I think not."

"Simon!" Claire struggled as he swung her up into his arms and stalked back to the stairs. He then started to climb. "What are you doing?"

"You're too tired to make rational decisions, so I'm making them for you."

"I'm never irrational."

"How controlled you are then, Miss Belmont, as I'm frequently irrational."

He carried her to the room he had recently left and climbed onto the bed with her still in his arms. He then lay back against the pillows.

"Simon—"

"What happened to start the sleeplessness, Claire? Talk to me."

"I can't sit here like this, in your arms." *No matter how much I want too.*

"Why not?"

"Don't be silly. It is not right that I do so."

"It is not right that we are alone in this house, just as it was not right we were alone in the carriage. So for tonight, do not worry about what is right."

Could she?

Plus, I'm bigger and stronger than you, and have had lots of sleep, Claire, so I have the upper hand. Now relax and tell me when this sleeplessness began."

He pulled her down on top of him so she lay on her side in his lap with her legs beside him on the bed. One of his hands then pressed her head into his chest as he had in the carriage.

"You're so different from other men I know."

"Different how?"

Claire placed her hand on his chest to feel his warmth and strength. "You are never afraid to get close to people, Simon, which is not the usual behavior of a nobleman. And I do not mean close in that way… you know."

"I know what you mean. Continue with what you were saying."

"You touch people when you are with them—a brush of fingers or a kiss on the cheek. You seem unaware of the boundaries most people have firmly erected around themselves, and for the most, people accept that in you because you are comfortable with it yourself. You use endearments freely, too, and I see the flush of pleasure on women's faces when you do. Tis not a criticism, you understand, Simon," Claire said quickly when he fell silent. She had always been secretly awed at how comfortable he seemed making those gestures and saying those words.

"I spent the early years of my life with no touching or endearments from my parents, Claire. My aunt and uncle visited briefly, and they would offer me love, yet it was only for a few days, and when they left I lived without it again. After my parent's deaths I went to live with my aunt and uncle, and it was then I understood what those gestures really mean to a person. I vowed never to live my life without them. Now tell me about your sleeplessness."

Claire did not ask him further questions about his childhood, as she sensed the memories were painful for him, but she wondered who would not want to touch this man or the boy he had once been.

"I was always a light sleeper yet I slept well until Anthony returned from war."

"Tell me about that?" His hand stroked her head in slow, sweeping motions that felt wonderful.

"When Anthony went away, I used to lie awake thinking about him and wondering if he would return. I still managed to sleep and it was not until he came home that the problems really started."

"Because he returned injured."

Claire felt the hot sting of tears as she nodded, her cheek rubbing over his chest. She hated crying yet when she thought of Anthony she couldn't stop herself. "Yes, and he suffered so much. Sometimes the pain was terrible, and he would clench his hands into fists to stop himself crying out. But the nights were the worst."

"And because you were awake, you kept him company?"

"He died in my arms. My beautiful brother went to war a strong and healthy man and came back broken."

"And after he died, you could not sleep?" Simon said softly.

"For so long, I saw him every time I closed my eyes."

"Have you ever taken laudanum?"

His fingers were stroking her hair, and brushing her cheek occasionally, and the feeling was heavenly. "I think Plimley puts it in the tisane he gives me occasionally, but it is only a very small amount, and I wake feeling horrid."

"I'm glad. Prolonged use is not good for you."

"Yes." Claire sighed, closing her eyes because they felt so heavy.

"What happens when you get into bed and close your eyes? What stops you from sleeping, Claire?"

"My head is suddenly filled with thoughts. They tumble around and around, keeping me awake. The harder I try to sleep, the more alert I feel. I get so frustrated and angry because I cannot control it."

"Surely your mother and Mathew—"

"They don't know," Claire whispered.

He ran one long finger down her cheek. His touch was so light, yet she felt it through her entire body.

"Why doesn't your family know, Claire?"

"I have no wish to worry my mother, as there is nothing she can do for me, and I have not discussed it with Mathew as I'm not close with him."

"As you were with Anthony?"

"Yes." She sighed again. Thinking of Mathew made Claire feel sad. He would never forgive her for this.

"Am I right in saying your inability to control your ability to sleep makes you want to control everything else in your life? The ever-competent Miss Belmont."

"You're very astute for a man."

She heard the rumble of laughter against her ear. "I don't know if I should be flattered or insulted."

"The thing is, Simon, I need to be in control because I fear if I wasn't, I would never leave the house. I do get sleep but not a lot, and some days, just getting dressed seems too much of an effort. I am continually worried I will fall asleep somewhere—a play, a musical."

"I cannot believe you have managed to fool us all for so long. Truly, it is a feat, especially as you never look anything but beautiful. Your face never shows fatigue."

"People only see what they want, Simon, and most evenings, all the women are looking at is my dress and jewelry and men, well—"

"They're looking at your lovely breasts."

"I can't believe you said that." She was too tired to sound outraged.

"You should be treading the boards, my dear Miss Belmont. A woman with your acting skills would be famous in no time."

"I would be hopeless at remembering my lines, I'm afraid. I have to re-read everything." Lord, his fingers felt glorious as he slipped them beneath her hair and rubbed her neck.

"There I would be able to help you. I'm brilliant at remembering things. In fact, I know none better. Perhaps we could form a team?"

She could hear the strong beat of his heart beneath her cheek. His skin was warm, and the hand stroking her, slow and steady. Before Claire realized what was happening, she felt herself being pulled down into sleep.

CHAPTER TEN

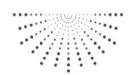

She woke disoriented. There was daylight coming in through the open curtains, and she distinctly remembered closing her eyes to darkness, yet she could recall nothing in between. Moreover, this was not her room, and there was something warm beneath her cheek. Opening her eyes, she saw a smooth expanse of skin and a dark nipple. Dear lord, she'd slept the night on Simon's chest. Tilting her head back, she looked up at his face, and sleepy grey eyes looked down at her.

"How do you feel?" His voice was husky, he looked like sin, and Claire had the ridiculous urge to climb on top of him and place her lips on his.

"I… uh, I—"

"Speechless, Claire? How delightful. I must remember to embarrass you when you attack me in the future."

"I slept, Simon," Claire whispered, realizing just what she had done. "Really slept."

"Yes you did, clever girl, and there is no need for embarrassment. However, there will be a payment for using me as a mattress."

She tried to get off him, placing her hand on his chest but he placed his over it so she couldn't move. "Release me, Simon."

"Payment first." He turned her on her back and loomed over her.

"Wh-what are you doing?"

"Are you ticklish, Claire? Shall we test that famous control of yours?"

"What? No, don't you dare!" she cried as his hands moved over her body in a way that made her giggle and squirm. "Stop, please, Simon!" No one had tickled her for years—in fact, since her childhood. "Th…this is improper," she stammered, trying to slap his hands aside.

"Well, well, not quite so controlled, after all, are we, Miss Belmont?"

Claire looked up at him as he grew still.

"You're beautiful in the morning, Claire."

They looked at each other silently for long, heated seconds, and then his body pressed hers into the mattress.

"Simon," Claire whispered, her hand reaching up to touch his face, mapping its contours as their gaze remained locked. Slowly, he lowered his head until their lips met. His body held her still, and his hands cupped her head as he took her mouth on a sensual journey that had Claire's head reeling in seconds. He explored her gently, teasing her lips as he placed one hot, lingering kiss after another on her mouth, and Claire could think of nothing but him. He surrounded her, the planes of his solid chest pressed against her breasts, his thighs trapped hers, and the feeling of being surrounded by him was exquisite.

"Christ, Claire, we have to stop." Simon's words were ragged as he tore his mouth from hers. Slipping his arms around her body, he held her close—so close, she could feel the thud of his heart against her own. It was wonderful to be held like this. It was almost as if they were one person. The feeling of being safe and cocooned—the wonder of it—felt so good.

"I have to leave the room now, Claire." His voice was a rasp as he eased away from her and climbed off the bed. She watched as he found his shirt. His muscles rippled as he pulled it over his head, and then she could see no more of that wonderful golden skin.

"Simon, what we just did… it was wrong. But I can never thank you enough for helping me sleep last night."

He didn't turn to look at her. Instead he made for the door. "The enjoyment was not all on your side, Claire, I assure you."

Letting himself out of the room, Simon closed the door and quickly headed outside. Finding a trough of water, he plunged his hands inside, and then when that did not cool his ardor, he submerged his head. God, he was on fire. Waking with her in his arms had created a furnace of need inside him. His body was hard from their kisses, and the feel of her breasts against his chest would be etched there forever. He'd done the right thing by stopping. He knew that even if his body did not. She'd said what they'd done was wrong, yet he could not deny how right it had felt.

They would be together for days, and she trusted him. He would not break that trust now. "Distance," Simon muttered before plunging his head back into the water. He must keep his distance.

He'd realized as he'd held her last night that he wanted Claire Belmont very much. Waking with her soft body pressed against his chest was exquisite torture, and the look of wonder in her brown eyes when she'd realized she had slept all night was something he would remember for a long time. When he'd turned her beneath him, his intentions had only been to make her smile, but that had all changed as he'd touched her. Suddenly he'd wanted to strip off that prim nightdress and fist one hand in her curls while he parted her thighs and drove inside her. He would need to be strong in the coming days, because Simon wasn't sure if he had her in his arms again that he would be able to walk away.

In one day, he had learned much about her. Her life was a play she enacted to keep the secret of her sleeplessness at bay. He admired her strength. Few could cope with so little sleep, but she did so masterfully.

Looking to the doorway, he saw it was still empty, so he made his way around the house and down the little path he knew so well to where the gardens lay. A riot of color greeted him. He felt the last of his tension ease as he walked down the path, studying the plants and shrubs he had bedded with his own hands. Bending occasionally, he pulled a weed or dead leaf, and then he stopped to inspect a rose he had planted not long ago.

"This is not the right place for you, my friend. We need to move you before you give up completely." Simon bent to dig in the loose soil with his bare hands, making a wide trench around the plant. He then dug deeper and eased the roots free.

"Why do you have your hands in the dirt, Simon?"

His fingers stilled before he looked up at Claire, who was almost upon him. He had not heard her approach because he was focused on the rose. "Uh—"

"Why have you dug a little trench around that plant?"

"It needs moving. The light is not right for it here."

He could feel her eyes on the back of his head as he continued to ease the plant free. Why did he suddenly feel as if he knelt before her, stripped of all his clothing? She had been vulnerable yesterday, today it was his turn.

"The owner of this house is quite the gardener, Simon. Do you know him well?"

It was a simple question, yet Claire Belmont rarely asked a question without a purpose.

"The gardens here are beautiful," she added when he did not answer.

"Yes they are." Standing, Simon carried the little bush to where it would be happy and then bent to dig a hole to place it in.

"What type of rose is that?"

"Old Blush," Simon said shortly, hoping she would simply walk back up the path and let him settle the little plant in its new bed.

"Does the owner not mind you digging about in his garden and uprooting his plants?"

He finished what he was doing, then patted the soil into place. He could almost hear the rose thanking him, sighing in relief. "Just ask the question, Claire," he said, standing to look at her. Surrounded by his flowers, she looked like the most beautiful bloom of them all. Morning sun stood at her back, and he could see the outline of her long, slender limbs through the skirts of her pale rose dress.

"Sometimes when the moon is bright and I struggle to sleep, I go to our gardens in London and pull weeds. It helps to calm me, and often I take a blanket and just sit there and enjoy the peace the garden offers," she said.

Simon didn't tell people his garden was his passion because most would not believe him. He wasn't ashamed, he just couldn't be bothered with the questions he suspected would arise. Looking at Claire, he could see she was genuine in what she had said.

"Who owns this house, Simon?"

"I do."

"And are you also responsible for the beauty that is all around us?"

He felt a rush of pleasure at the knowledge that she thought his gardens beautiful. He spent a few seconds brushing the dirt off his hands while he worked through his answer. "It is something I have always liked to do." He caught her scent as she moved closer—a subtle blend of rose and honeysuckle, both flowers he loved.

"I would say you love doing it, Simon," she added, looking around her. She then bent to pull a weed that had wound itself around the stem of a flower. Standing, she presented it to him.

"Why, Miss Belmont, how sweet of you."

"I am all that is sweet, Lord Kelkirk."

He snorted at the falsehood. "Of course you are. It was someone completely different who told me my waistcoat was better suited to hang in your windows than from my body." He turned, making his way to the small shed at the rear, where he found water. Washing his hands, he then scooped some out in the old cup he left beside it and carried it back to where Claire and his rose waited. Dropping to his knees he poured the water around the plant.

"To be fair, had I known of your love of color," she said, sweeping her hand in a half circle, "I would not have been so critical."

"That waistcoat received numerous compliments."

"From women only, I imagine—women who wanted to insinuate themselves into your good graces."

Leaving the cup on the ground, Simon stood and closed the distance between them. She looked right standing here in his garden. "The Earl of Dobbie liked it."

She snorted. "The Earl of Dobbie is too old to know better."

"Daniel told me Eva wanted a dress made of the exact

material, which should probably have been an indication that you were indeed correct in your dislike of it."

She giggled, and the sound reminded Simon of her lying beneath him on the bed whilst he'd tickled her. Clearing his throat as his body stirred to life again, he suggested they return to the house and prepare to leave.

"Were these gardens the result of my hands, I would be very proud, Simon." She said the words over her shoulder so did not see his smile.

"Thank you. Now tell me how do you feel after your night's sleep?"

"Wonderful, which is probably not how I should be feeling, considering what I am about to do. However I do feel that way. My eyes are not scratchy, and my limbs are not heavy. I feel ten years younger, Simon. Thank you."

"It is a chore, to be sure, but it seems I will have to sleep with you every night from this day forward just to ensure you get a restful night's sleep." She laughed, as she was meant to. "Now if you pack your things, Claire, I shall rouse my lazy coachmen, and we shall get back on the road."

They talked of plants, and she demanded he tell her all the varieties of roses he knew. After stopping for something to eat at a small inn, they were soon again on the road. Claire again started questioning him, this time asking him how many species of flowers he could name, to which he replied lots and far too many to mention.

They played word games as the carriage rolled on and then sat in companionable silence until he fell asleep, as he always did when he was in a carriage for too long.

Simon woke once again looking at Claire. He could get used to waking up looking at her. She was far prettier than his valet.

"You should bring a stick, then you could poke me when I nod off," he said yawning.

"The idea has merits, however I also enjoy the silence," she said looking out the window.

"Because I rattle on so much?" Simon teased stretching his arms, trying to work out some of the knots he had received from being trapped inside a small space for too long.

"Exactly so," she said looking out the window once more.

Lifting the hatch above his head he instructed Merlin to leave the main road to Liverpool and find a quiet, less frequented inn to stop at for the night, where he hoped they would not run into anyone they knew. The chances were unlikely, as the London season was at its height, yet he would not take that risk.

As the miles passed, Simon watched Claire grow quieter as dusk began to fall. She had stopped talking completely by the time they pulled to a halt outside a small establishment.

"It will be all right, Claire." Simon took her hands. "We will pretend you are my wife tonight, as this will give you protection and put us in the same room. I will take the chair or the floor," he added as she opened her mouth to argue, as he knew she would.

"All right. If you think that is best."

He was surprised at her agreement but did not comment, instead leading her inside.

"I wish for two rooms, please—one for my wife and I and another for my coachmen."

The proprietor had narrow eyes, to Simon's mind. However he was clean, and from the little he had seen, his establishment appeared to be, too.

"Your men can sleep in the stables."

"I want my men in the room next to my wife and I," Simon said politely. "If you have a problem with that, sir, we shall find somewhere else that does not."

The man grumbled and then nodded for them to follow him.

"I want a private parlor, also," Simon added, hearing loud voices coming from somewhere inside the place, "and a meal set out, if you please. Plus warm water for bathing. Again, I will pay for these privileges."

Their room overlooked the courtyard below and appeared clean enough. It held a chair, a bed, and a rug on the floor.

"If you could have tea l readied, sir, I will bring my wife down shortly," Simon said to the man before he left.

"Yes, my lord."

Claire had wandered toward the window and was looking down below.

"Come, we shall have some tea and await the fine evening meal I'm sure the proprietor is now conjuring up for us," he said, holding out his hand to her.

"I think I should just stay in here, Simon."

"It is a private parlor, so you will be safe," Simon said, watching her fidget with the curtain. "Now tell me, besides the fact that you have lied to your family and are about to go to Liverpool to pick up your brother's illegitimate child, what else is bothering you, Claire?"

"This is wrong, Simon."

She was looking down at the courtyard, but he suspected she was not really seeing it. "What is wrong?"

"You helping me, being here with me. I have put you to so much trouble and this is not your problem. My selfishness could bring so much trouble down on your head." She turned now, and he saw once again that her brown eyes were filled with worry.

"I thought we'd dealt with that matter, Claire. It is my choice to help you and one I make gladly. Now please take my hand, wife, as I'm hungry and have no time for your vapors."

She gave him one jerky nod, then came across the room and slipped her hand inside his. He led them silently down the stairs to the small parlor the landlord had prepared.

They ate the bland meal of potatoes and beef in a thin gravy. He talked, and she listened but offered only the occasional reply.

Merlin arrived as they finished. The coachman bowed stiffly to Claire before speaking. "There are a few shady characters at present in the public rooms, my lord. Ben and I thought to alert you to that fact," Merlin said, shooting Claire a quick, worried look.

"Thank you, Merlin. I shall take Miss Belmont upstairs now, and I would ask that you and Ben also retire soon. We shall be safe until morning with you beside us."

Merlin didn't question that Claire would stay in the same room as Simon because Simon had informed his men that for her safety, this would be the case. If they thought it odd, neither said so, and he paid them handsomely for that loyalty.

"I'll get Ben to finish his ale, my lord, and we'll be up shortly."

"Excellent. Come now, Claire, we shall retire," Simon said when Merlin had left. She didn't argue, just took his hand once more, and let him lead her out of the dining parlor.

"Evening, my lord, my lady. Fine night, ain't it?"

The man who had spoken appeared before them, a foolish, drunken smile displaying two yellow teeth on his face. His clothes were dirty, and his breath smelt of many hours' drinking.

"Good evening. Please step aside, as you are blocking our way." Simon kept Claire behind him while he held his eyes steady on the man. "I have no qualms about making you step aside if that is the problem, sir, however I would rather not do so with my wife watching."

The man looked at him, and something in Simon's face alerted him that it would be in his best interests to move, so he did, muttering something as he shuffled away.

Simon urged Claire up the stairs and into their room, where he closed the door behind him. Looking in the lock, he found no key and cursed soundly. Pulling the pistol from his belt, he handed it to Claire.

"Hold this until I come back with the key. If anyone enters, shoot him… unless it's me or one of my coachman," he added with a smile she failed to return. "I'll keep you safe, Claire—trust me."

"But who will keep you safe, Simon? Must you go downstairs with that man there?" She was pale again, and he wondered if she was thinking that all of this could have been happening to her alone, with no one to look after her. The thought did not sit well in his stomach so it must have been terrifying to her.

"I have two of my men at present down there. They will keep me safe whilst I get the key from the proprietor. I will be five minutes at the most, Claire, I promise."

She nodded, and Simon left making his way downstairs. The proprietor was behind the bar. Merlin and Ben were nowhere in sight, which he guessed meant they were checking the horses before retiring.

"I wish for the key to my room, please, sir. I do not want to sleep the night with the door unlocked."

"Lookee here, Neb. It's the toff what I found in the hallway. Right shame he don't have the sweet filly with him."

Simon ignored the voice over his right shoulder and the sudden need to plant his fist in the man's face and continued to look at the proprietor. He needed to get back to Claire, and starting a fight was not the way to achieve that.

"I believe I asked you for something, sir. Perhaps now would be the time for you to retrieve it?"

"Thinks he's too grand for us, he does, Neb. One of them toffs with full pockets that would fall if a body blew on him."

"Now," Simon said with deadly calm to the proprietor. The man saw the threat in his eyes and quickly hurried away to retrieve the key. Only then did Simon turn to see what he was to face.

CHAPTER ELEVEN

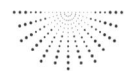

Where are you, Simon?

Opening the door, Claire put her head outside and listened. She heard lots of noise, but she didn't think any of it came from Simon. Holding the gun in one hand, she thought about taking the candle with her to light the way, but that would leave her with no hands free, so instead, she made her way to the stairs and slowly down until she could hear the noise coming from the rear of the building. It was loud and sounded as though glass was being smashed. Then she heard the sickening thud of a fist hitting flesh. Simon would be furious with her for coming down here. However if he was in trouble, she needed to help him, because the trouble he was in was her fault. Edging closer, Claire saw the door had a glass panel in it, so she looked through. Men were fighting—lots of men. Searching the group, she managed to find Simon, Merlin and Ben. It appeared they were being set upon by all the rest of the men in the room. While she watched, Simon took a blow to the face that rocked him back on his heels.

"Best you go up to your room, my lady."

Claire spun to face the proprietor, who spoke behind her.

"Get in there!" she shrieked, making him wince. "Stop this at once, they are killing my husband and coachman!"

The proprietor chuckled. "Won't be any death, my lady, just a good milling. And your man seems to have a way of handling himself you don't often see in a nobleman."

"Give me that key, you bloody coward!" Snatching what she hoped was her room key out of his hand, she opened the door and lifted the gun.

"Stop or I'll shoot!"

No one took any notice of her as she yelled loudly while waving the gun about. Claire's eyes fell on a chair, so she stepped up onto it and then onto the table beside. She picked up the glass tumbler at her feet, then dropped it on the ground as hard as she could. The men did not stop. A few turned to look at her, but then carried on fighting, so she lifted another glass and threw it as hard as she could at all the bottles lined up behind the bar. Several smashed and this time the loud noise drew plenty of attention. Slowly every man in the room stopped what they were doing and turned to look at her.

Raising the pistol, she then pointed it at the man who had punched Simon. "You will all leave this establishment at once," Claire said. Bracing her legs, she locked her trembling knees and held the gun with both hands once more. "I asked you to do something, gentlemen," she added when no one moved. "Now I insist you do it, or I will fire, and as I watched you plant your fist in my husband's face, you will be the first to receive my bullet… between the legs," Claire added slowly. She watched the man's color recede as he looked at where she was aiming.

"Christ!"

This was from Simon, but she didn't look his way.

Instead, she held the man's gaze. It was he that lowered his first.

"Everyone out now!"

Behind her, the proprietor had finally made his way inside and was starting to order people from his establishment.

"Give me the gun now, my lady."

Claire looked down at Merlin, who appeared at her feet, holding out a hand. She placed the gun gently in his palm. She noticed his lip was split and his nose bloodied. This was her fault. These three men had been hurt protecting her. Guilt sat like a heavy weight on her shoulders.

"I'm sorry," she whispered, looking from him to Ben, and then lastly, Simon, because she knew seeing his beautiful face bruised and bloodied would hurt her the most. "This is my fault." She watched Simon walk toward her, his eyes never leaving her face. There was blood on his cheek, and one of his eyes was slowly darkening. "Dear god, Simon, I'm sorry," she choked out.

He didn't speak, just placed his hands on her waist and lifted her to the ground, pulling her into his chest briefly before taking her hand. She heard him speak to his men, and then he led her from the room. Simon pushed her back up the stairs and into their room.

"I…uh, I have the key, Simon."

He took it from her silently and then locked the door. She moved to the window while he slowly pulled off his jacket, wincing as he did so.

"There is water. I will wash the… the blood from you, Simon."

He removed his boots and shirt. Only then did he look at her. Rage had darkened his eyes to the color of a stormy night.

"I told you to stay in here, Claire. Merlin told you there

were unsavory men about the place, yet still you came downstairs. Do you know what could have happened?" His words were clipped and cold.

"I had your gun."

"And that is supposed to make me feel better, is it? A woman with a gun in a room full of men who have had too much to drink!"

"I know how to shoot a gun!" Claire defended herself.

He closed his eyes briefly. "You know how to shoot at targets, not men, Claire. Believe me, there is a difference."

"I'm sorry you believe what I did was foolish, yet I would do it again, Simon. You were in that room taking a beating because of me. Had I not coerced you into this, then you would be sipping lemonade at Almack's tonight."

"I was not taking a beating," he said slowly, and this, Claire suspected, was because it hurt his jaw to talk. "In fact, we fared quite well. Nor did I say your actions were foolish. They were brave. Unnecessary, however. And were I to choose between Almack's insipid lemonade and a good mill, I would choose the latter any day."

Claire did not speak again because she knew he was lying and trying to make her feel better. She got the water and a piece of cloth and carried it to where he now sat on the bed. She then gently cleaned his bruised and bloodied face. There was swelling around one eye, and bruises were starting to form elsewhere. He did not move and gave only the occasional wince or grunt. When she was finished, he laid on the bed with a sigh.

"Should I tend your men, Simon?"

"They will tend themselves or find someone to do it, Claire. Lie down now and we shall try to get some sleep. We are to leave early."

There was knock on the door, so Claire asked who it was and then opened it when the landlord answered. He handed her a small tray, which held a bottle, glass, and some ointment he said his wife had given him. He looked contrite, but Claire didn't thank him because she was still angry, and the truth was, he was probably more worried about receiving payment for their night's accommodation than fretting over Simon's wounds. Instead, she nodded and told him to make sure their men received the proper care.

"Here, Simon. This will help you sleep," she said, pouring him a large glass of whatever was in the bottle. Lifting his head, he took it, swallowed the contents in one gulp, and then lay back down. "I'll just put this ointment on your scrapes now." His eyes stayed on hers as she smoothed it over his cheek and the small cut under his eye. Then, taking a deep breath, she rubbed it into the bruising over his ribs. His skin felt warm beneath her fingers, and the only reaction he gave to her touch was the occasional twitch. However, he kept his steady gaze on her face until she finished.

"Now lie down so I can sleep, Claire. I can't do so with you standing there."

"I'll take the chair."

Claire was suddenly lifted off her feet. "Simon, you're hurt!" He rested her beside him, one of his hands on her wrist, anchoring her to his side.

"Sleep, woman."

She didn't point out that she still had all her clothes on, nor that she had no hope of sleeping this night. She just lay still until she was sure he slept. Only then did Claire rise and go to the chair. The candle had burnt low, but still there was enough light to see the bruises forming on his body. She couldn't do this to him, or his drivers anymore. This was her problem, not there's. She'd chosen this path, and now needed to walk it alone.

Quietly, Claire opened the larger of her bags and pulled out the old black cape and bonnet she had used when venturing into Tuttle Lane. Taking Simon's gun, she tucked it into the pocket of the cape. Picking up both bags, she then threw him one last look before leaving the room.

He would come after her—she knew that—but if she could reach Liverpool before Simon and collect the child, then hopefully she would make it back to London before him. It was a risk leaving alone but one she was willing to take. If he caught her, she would face the consequences, but Claire hoped she did not have to face him again until she was safely back in London.

The proprietor was busy picking up broken bottles when she approached him, and she suspected it was his wife helping him. Claire was pleased to hear the woman censuring him loudly and at length about the night's events.

"Can we help you, my lady?" The man addressed her.

"I have need of a carriage and a driver at once. I have no wish to explain further. I will give you a hefty purse if you simply see to this immediately for me."

She lifted the pouch from her bodice and shook it.

"Will your man be angered with me in the morning if I do this?" The proprietor had a calculating look in his eyes as he studied the pouch.

"He will not," she lied, "and the money in here should make up for any difficulties that arise."

"I have only a cart to take you."

"That will suffice," Claire shot a worried look at the door behind her that led upstairs. If Simon walked through it now, she would be in large amounts of trouble.

"And where are you wanting to be taken?"

"I wish to either hire a carriage to take me to Liverpool, or one that will take me to where I can catch the stage."

The man nodded. "Very well. I'll have you taken to the next village where you can catch the stage, but it will cost you."

Claire opened the purse and began to count out the money until the man said stop. Looking at what she had left, her heart sank. How was she to pay for a carriage to Liverpool and back to London with this? And what if whoever held the child demanded money before handing it to her? Tucking the considerably lighter purse back into her bodice, Claire realized she would have to catch the stage to Liverpool and then think about her next move when she reached her destination.

Following the man outside, she was soon seated on the hard bench seat of the cart, beside his son. His name was Henry and he was sixteen. She apologized for his lack of sleep, and he shrugged.

"Taint no mind to me, my lady. I enjoy getting away from there, and I won't be back until tomorrow, so someone else has to do me chores now."

He didn't say much of anything else. However she discovered during the long night they spent together that he did like to sing. Often when Claire was nervous or unsettled, she hummed, and as she did, Henry had started to sing. He had the voice of an angel, and as the little cart rumbled slowly along the rutted roads, they sang every song they knew and many Claire didn't.

Simon remained steady in her thoughts, and every now and again she would turn to look behind her into the dark, but the road stayed empty.

The moon was low, but Henry seemed to know where he was going, so she tucked the blanket he had given her around her body, and sang along with him until, just as dawn had started to break, they rolled into a village.

"If you go over there," Henry said, pointing to a tall white building that had a large black sign with a goat on it, "you can book for the next stage at The Goat."

"Well, thank you, Henry, for the ride and for the singing.

I'm sure I will remember this night and your lovely voice for many years to come."

He blushed to his ears when she kissed his cheek, then he handed her the bags he'd pulled out of the back of his cart. Bobbing his head, he led his cart back up the road and disappeared. Claire hoped he and his pony would have a rest and something to eat before attempting the return journey.

Squaring her shoulders, she fought the sudden urge to call him back. "You are a intelligent woman, Claire Belmont, you can do this." Bolstered by these words, she began making her way toward The Goat. As it was still early, there were only a few people on the streets, and none were bothering to look at her. The stench of ale hit her as she entered the inn minutes later, and visions of last night filled her head. Simon would wake sore and bruised today, and when he found her missing, he would also be furious. Claire had seen him angry last night, but she knew his anger toward her today would be far worse.

"Can I help you?"

"I wish to purchase a seat on the stage to Liverpool, please. When are you expecting it to arrive?" Her heart sank when the woman said not until late afternoon.

"May I stay here and wait for it?" Claire asked, forcing a smile onto her face.

"You can take a chair, but you have to buy a meal."

She wasn't sure what a chair had to do with purchasing a meal, but she handed over more of her precious money anyway.

"You can wait through there," the woman pointed her to a room that had people sleeping on the floor. Taking up her bags once more, she walked over slumbering bodies to a chair beside the window facing the street. Placing her bags at her feet, Claire then folded her hands in her lap. At least if she sat there, she would see if Simon appeared and have time to hide. Looking around the room, Claire realized that were something to happen to her she was completely alone, as no one would know where she was. Which of course, was what she wanted. She had to reach Liverpool, and had to do it in the time allotted to her by that letter. She must do this for Anthony.

SIMON WOKE WITH A GROAN. His eye was swollen shut, and his face hurt like hell. Moving slowly so as not to wake Claire, he turned onto his side and eased himself upright to sit on the edge of the bed. He pressed his ribs and concluded they were bruised more than broken. His nose did not make any crunching noises upon being tweaked, so he suspected that was good, too. Rising, he moved like an old man to the water, and then, cupping it in his hand, he washed his face. The water felt blissful. Simon wondered how his coachmen were faring. They had arrived minutes after the fight started and waded in with smiles on their faces. Drying his own face, he looked briefly to the window. It was just getting light. He would need to wake Claire so they could leave as soon as they'd eaten. One more night and they should reach Liverpool. Hopefully, tonight would not be quite so eventful.

His eyes went to the bed and found it empty. He searched the room and found her bags gone. "Stupid, idiotic, bloody woman!" He roared these words so loud that in seconds, Merlin was pounding at his door. In two strides, he had it opened. "Miss Belmont appears to have taken the notion into her head to continue this journey on her own. Get the horses ready to leave at once."

Simon grabbed his clothes and pulled them on. Reaching for his gun, he noted it was gone and raised his eyes to the roof. Picking up his luggage, he then left the room, slamming the door so loudly, it shook the walls.

"Where is my wife?" Simon found the proprietor in the kitchen with a woman who was presumably his own wife. Both looked at him in wide-eyed terror as he stormed in. "Answer the bloody question, or last night's mess will seem like a tea party compared to what I will do to your establishment."

"Our son drove her in his cart to catch the stage to Liverpool, my lord."

"In a cart!" Simon cursed again, this time dredging up a few words he normally used only when alone. "And did you not think letting a young woman leave here with only one man for company would be dangerous?"

"Henry knows the shortcuts, my lord. People rarely travel those roads."

"How much did she pay you?"

The proprietor edged closer to his wife, bloody coward that he was. "A great deal, my lord."

Simon had never wanted to hit someone more than he did right now. However, his knuckles were raw and his body ached. Furthermore, he needed to get to Claire before she fell into more trouble. "How long ago did she leave?" The words were snapped out as quickly as a bullet fired from a gun.

"Last night—not long after you retired, my lord."

But she was in a cart that would travel much slower than he could, Simon calculated. "Draw me a map with the route they took, and be quick about it."

"Can't say as I can write or draw, my lord."

Simon exhaled slowly. "Tell me the roads he took, then."

The man stuttered out several words, one on top of the other, which Simon tried and failed to decipher. Just as he was about to wrap his fingers around his neck, the wife elbowed the fool aside and told him in a clear voice what he wanted to know. Without another word, Simon turned on his heel and stalked away.

His carriage was waiting, and he retold the directions to his drivers, both of whom had colorful bruises to match his. "They're in a cart, so we should catch them before they reach their destination, if not just as they arrive. His men merely nodded, obviously noting the look of fury burning behind his eyes. "Go as fast as you can, Merlin. I fear for her safety if left alone too long."

"We'll get to her before trouble strikes, my lord."

Nodding, Simon felt a small grain of reassurance from his stoic coachman's words. Climbing inside, he then prayed.

They traveled roads that were not well used, so the journey was not a comfortable one for a man whose body was bruised and sore. His ribs hurt. His face ached, and when they hit a rut and he was forced to grip the strap above his head to steady himself, his knuckles protested furiously.

"I will shake you, Claire Belmont, until your teeth rattle. Then I will sit you across from me and lecture you for hours," he muttered. Christ, was she safe? Had she already fallen on trouble?

Closing his eyes, he rested his aching head on the back of the seat while bracing his boots on the one opposite. He could see her as she had looked last night, standing on that table, his gun braced in her hands and that ferocious look on her flushed face. She'd been ready to take them all on, every man in the room, and each one, Simon was sure, had envied him at that moment. She'd stood there with her pretty dress on and demanded every man, but the three that belonged to her, leave.

"God, Claire, where are you?" Pulling the curtain aside, he searched the paddocks and trees as if she would suddenly appear. Fear gnawed at his insides, and that made his anger climb.

She was so much more than he'd ever believed her to be. She

RESCUED BY A VISCOUNT

was loyal, and he now knew would do what it took to protect those she felt needed protection. Not that he had ever doubted her, but still, at that moment when he'd seen her standing on that table ready to fight for him, through his horror, he had felt a large, warm weight settle in his chest. She'd been there for him and his men, and there were not many people in Simon's life who would have taken such a risk to secure his safety.

She'd tended his cuts and bruises and plied him with spirits, and he'd then fallen asleep, and the little witch had left him. Had she thought he would wake and see her gone and just shrug? Simply make his way back to London and let her continue alone?

Foolish woman.

Simon didn't know how long they had been traveling before he felt the carriage slow, and stop. He had the door open and was outside in seconds.

"The cart there, my lord. I think that's it."

Following Ben's hand, he saw they had entered a village, and coming down the main street was a cart driven by a young boy.

"Why do you think that's it, Ben? Surely, there is more than one cart in this village."

"I saw that horse in the stall next to ours yesterday, my lord."

"Good enough," Simon said. "Ben, you get food for all of us, and Merlin, you take care of the horses. I will meet you at that stable." He pointed to a large building that had horses milling about in front of it.

Simon walked across the street toward the cart, which had to stop or go around him. It stopped. "Where is the woman you brought here?"

The boy looked at him silently for several seconds.

"I mean her no harm, Boy."

He nodded and then lifted his hand, pointing to a large, two-storied establishment further down the road.

"Has the stage been through today?"

"No, my lord. I've been here many hours and it has not arrived yet."

Nodding, Simon stepped to the side, then made his way to the establishment called The Goat. He entered and walked slowly from room to room. She was in the last. Relief nearly buckled his knees as he saw her sitting alone in the corner with her bags at her feet. She wore a black bonnet and cape, presumably the same ones he'd seen her in that day in the lane. Around her, people chatted and laughed while she slept. Her head rested on the back of the seat, hands neatly folded in her lap. Unlike last night, when she had appeared fire and brimstone, she now looked small and vulnerable again. He walked across the room, nodding to people as they moved out of his way. He suspected this was due to his battered face and ferocious scowl. Reaching her, Simon had an urge to haul her into his arms and hold her. However he was still furious, so he nudged her shoulder with his hand instead.

She woke suddenly, sitting upright in the chair, eyes wide and unfocused as she looked up at him. Blinking several times, she then looked around the room, as if to remind herself where she was, and then back at him.

"Simon." One word but it sounded wrenched from deep inside her.

"Follow me outside, Claire. If you don't, I will throw you over my shoulder and make a scene bigger than any you have ever witnessed." Simon picked up her luggage and walked toward the door instead of following his impulse and scooping her into his arms. He knew she followed, because he heard her apologizing as she passed people.

"Simon, please…"

He ignored her, instead making his way outside and

then starting back down the road toward where his carriage awaited. She surprised him by cursing, but still he did not stop. Walking into the stables, he located his carriage.

"Load these, please, Merlin." Simon handed Claire's luggage to him and then opened the carriage door.

"Why won't you at least listen to me, Simon?"

She now stood beside him, looking up at him from under the brim of that ugly black bonnet. Her brown eyes were wary, and he knew she was scared, yet she didn't back down.

"Get in," Simon said, pointing inside the carriage.

"No."

He wouldn't laugh. He was too angry for that, even if she looked delectable defying him. "Claire, the pain in my body is not making me amiable. Therefore it would be in your best interests to do as I say and do it quickly."

"It is best I go alone, Simon, surely after last night you can see that? This is my problem, not yours."

"For the love of god," he muttered, picking her up. He stepped up into the carriage and threw her on the seat with perhaps a bit more force than necessary. Sitting near the door, he slammed it shut, trapping her inside. "I've told you I want to come with you. I've told you it is my choice, and still you take the foolish notion into your head to flee in the middle of the night, thus, in your eyes, protecting me."

"It was for the best," she said defiantly, crossing her arms.

"For whom? Did you believe I would wake to find you gone and think, well that's that, then. Claire's gone—I shall now return to London and enjoy the season?" Simon's voice was a furious growl as he glared at her. "You thought I wouldn't worry what had become of you? That I would not wonder if you'd made it to Liverpool to collect the child? And what if trouble had befallen you? Who would have known where you were? Certainly not your family, as they believe you are safely nestled at Stratton with your dearest friend."

His words made the color leech from her face.

"Think with your head, Claire. Think rationally before doing anything else rash, I beg of you."

Tears fell silently down her cheeks as she looked at him. "I don't want you hurt anymore, Simon. I couldn't bear it. I thought if I reached Liverpool and collected the child, I could be back in London before you caught up with me."

"Do you know what would hurt me more than these?" he asked, lifting a hand to the bruises on his face.

"No." Her voice was husky as she wiped away tears with her gloves.

"Hearing that some man had hurt you, or that you were lost and alone with no one to turn to. Those things would hurt more than any pain a fist could cause."

She pressed her hands into her eyes to try to stem the flow of tears.

"I have been cold with fear since I woke. Had the proprietor's wife not been beside him this morning when I confronted him, I would have, in all likelihood, killed him for letting you leave alone."

"You sh-should not be involved in this, Simon."

He blew out a loud sigh that made his ribs ache.

"I am involved, Claire. Why can't you see that?"

She started to say something, but instead, her words turned into a sob.

"I'm not leaving you. I will see you and the child safely back to London and it would be in your best interests to accept that," Simon said.

She wanted to talk, but every time she tried, another sob came out.

"Come here, Claire." Her tears were undoing him, causing his own eyes to itch. "Please," he added, holding out his arms to her. Suddenly, she flew at him, wrapping her arms around his neck and holding him close as she wept. And he, for the first time since she'd left him, felt peace. Nestling her into his body, they sat that way until Ben knocked on the door. Only then did he put her on the seat beside him. Opening the door, he took the food, and soon the carriage was once again on the road to Liverpool.

"Remove that offensive cape and bonnet, Claire. You look like you're in mourning," Simon said as he bit into a pie, the warm meat and gravy doing admirable things to restore his spirits.

She was too tired to fight him, so she first took off her gloves, then the bonnet, and finally, the cape.

"Eat this now, and then you can sleep."

Taking the pie, she looked at him. "Are you finished ordering me about?"

"No." Simon didn't smile as she rolled her eyes.

They ate in silence, then he grabbed her cape and bundled it into a pillow before placing it behind his head. Easing back against it, he let out a relieved sigh. "At least I have found a use for it." She tried to resist as he reached for her, but Simon simply wrapped both arms around her and settled her against his chest, where he knew she fit perfectly.

"Henry sang to me last night."

"Who's Henry?" Simon pulled the ribbon from her plait, and slowly unraveled it.

"The innkeeper's son. He had the voice of an angel."

Her words were sounding slurred now, as if she had been overindulging, and he knew in seconds, she would be asleep. "Let's hope he has his mother's brains, as well."

She snuffled into his chest. "It took me ages to plait that."

"I'll re-plait it. Now sleep, Claire."

"Will you sing to me, Simon?"

"No."

She gave a tired sigh and placed one hand over his heart. Minutes later, she was asleep. Simon smoothed her hair out and then, kissing the top her head, he joined her.

THAT NIGHT WAS SPENT at another inn. This one was very quiet, and the proprietor was happy to accommodate all of Simon's needs. Simon had a bath ordered for Claire and left the room to give her some privacy, although the maid had placed a screen around it. When he opened the door later, he felt his heart sink. The room was empty. "Claire!"

He heard splashing and gasping from behind the screen. Relieved, he pressed a hand to his chest, where it thudded uncomfortably.

"I fell asleep, Simon."

"You sound surprised by that," he said, making his way to a chair. He sat down and began pulling off his boots. He'd thought she'd run from him again.

"I... Yes, I am. I have never fallen asleep anywhere during the day." He heard the wonder in her voice. "Of course, I cannot vouch for my infant years."

"Perhaps after a few nights' sleep, your body and mind have begun to enjoy the state of slumber, and a habit is forming."

He could hear the sound of her rising and imagined the water running over her lush curves.

"Please ask the maid to bring you some hot water, Simon. I fear this is quite cold now."

Glad to leave the room with his heated thoughts, he did as she asked, only to return to find her sitting in her nightdress on the edge of the bed.

"Your face is a myriad of colors now, Simon. Is it painful?" She was attempting to brush her hair, which fell in damp coils to her waist. God, she looked like heaven, sitting there in that prim white nightdress.

"Simon?"

"Uh… yes, much better now, thank you."

The maids arrived and refilled the tub. Relieved, he slipped behind the screen to undress. Then he stepped into the water and began to scrub himself thoroughly, using a cloth. His skin was nearly raw by the time he stepped out, and his bruises ached, but he was no longer aroused.

"You take the bed, Claire. I will lay a blanket on the floor."

"But your body is still sore. Surely you would be better on the bed."

"I'm not letting you sleep on the floor, Claire." Rubbing the drying cloth over his head and body, Simon then pulled on his breeches and stepped out from behind the screen.

"Then we will share a bed once more, Simon. I know you are a gentleman… for the most," she added, blushing.

He watched her rise from the bed and move to the side, where she pulled back the covers and climbed in. Simon wasn't sure he could do the same. He knew what she felt like in his arms now, and that only made him want more. Part of him had always felt an attraction for Claire Belmont, but now it was a fire in his blood. Could he sleep next to her without reaching for her?

"If you sleep on the floor," she continued, "then we shall both have no sleep."

"How so, when you have the bed," Simon said, moving to the opposite side. He then doused the lamp and pulled back the covers. He could do this. He was a grown man who had control over his passions.

"I will worry about you, and that will keep me awake."

He settled himself and then turned onto his side to face her. However, she was facing the wall. "So this gesture of yours is not actually because you fear for my comfort—it is because you fear for your own?"

She snuffled. "Oh dear. It seems I have been found out."

He smiled into the dark and realized he could do this if it meant she would sleep. It was a nice feeling that she was relaxed enough in his company now to slumber, especially considering what they had just endured.

"Good night, Simon."

"Good night, Claire.

CHAPTER TWELVE

*S*imon woke to an elbow in his sore ribs. Struggling through the waves of sleep, he tried to establish what had happened.

"You should support me!"

"What?" Turning on his side, he blinked several times to clear his eyes.

"How can you do this, Mathew?"

Bracing himself on one elbow, Simon looked down at Claire. In the moonlight, he could see she was lying on her back, body rigid, arms waving around above her head. She still slept but was lecturing her brother while she did so.

"Be there for the child, if not for me. You were never there for me. So many long, dark, and lonely nights."

"It's all right, Claire. It's just a dream. Come on, wake up now." Simon cupped her cheek, turning her to face him.

"Simon?"

"Are there other men you use for a pillow?" He said the words softly, as slowly she focused on him.

"I was dreaming."

"Yes."

"I don't usually dream."

Simon pushed the hair off her face so she could see clearly. "Do you remember what your dream was about?"

"Mathew."

"You were angry with him."

She turned her face into his palm, and he heard her sigh. "Go back to sleep now, Simon. I'm sorry for waking you."

"Would you like to talk about it?"

"No." Just the one flat word, which Simon knew meant don't probe. He would, however, as soon as they had the child. Mathew Belmont would be made to face the reality of his brother's child if he had to beat him into submission.

He leaned down to kiss her, comfort her. Instead their lips met and held, clinging to each other.

"Claire?" Simon breathed her name as he lifted his head. Their mouths now inches apart. He didn't know what he was asking her, only that he wanted this woman with a desperation he'd never felt for anyone before.

Claire curled her fingers around Simon's neck, and urged his mouth down to hers. She'd wanted this since their last kiss. Needed to feel his big body pressed to hers again.

"We can't do this, Claire—not all of it." His words were hoarse and Claire heard the passion in them that matched her own.

"Make me feel what you did at your cottage, Simon, please."

Lowering his head, he kissed her again, slow and achingly sweet. He then moved to the skin above the neckline of her nightdress. Fire ignited wherever his mouth touched, and Claire was soon wrapped in the sensual spell that Simon was weaving around her. She felt his fingers on her leg, easing the hem of her nightdress higher. He stroked her thigh, caressing every inch of skin he uncovered.

"Undo your buttons, Claire."

She obeyed the rasped words. Her fingers fumbled, but finally managed what he asked, and then he was kissing the top of her breasts. Heat pooled inside her. Pressure built and she ached to have it released. He licked around her nipple as his hand reached the top of her thigh, hot strokes of his tongue driving her passion higher.

"Open your legs for me, sweetheart. Let me touch you."

She did as he asked, and then his fingers was there, stroking the curls. He slid one between the damp folds below and touched the hard bud. She moaned, her body arching beneath his, as Simon bit down softly on her nipple.

"Soon, Claire—not long now."

She had no idea what he spoke of, knew only that if he stopped she would be lost. And then he pushed his fingers inside her tight sheath as his teeth continued to torment her nipple, and she felt it, the beautiful burst of pleasure that left her shuddering seconds later.

"Dear god."

His laugh held little humor, and to Claire sounded as if he was in pain. Simon's face was tight with tension, and his teeth clenched.

"You did not receive pleasure like I, Simon."

"Tis best this way."

"No, I don't believe that. Let me give it to you."

"No, Claire. You are a innocent lady—"

"Therefore I cannot give a man pleasure?" Claire's heart still raced, yet her body felt languid. It was a wonderful feeling.

"It is not right."

Placing a hand on his chest, she tried pushed him onto his

back. "I may be innocent, yet I know you need relief, Simon, just as you gave it to me. So tell me what to do."

"No."

He got out of bed quickly, and looked down at her, his face tense. Claire rose too, kneeling on the edge. Not giving herself time to think about what she was doing, she pressed one hand against his erection.

"Claire, don't—"

She ran it up and down stroking him through his breeches. He twitched and then moaned so she did it again.

Hardly believing she dared to do such a thing, Claire undid the buttons, and opened his breeches. Taking the hot, hard length into her hands, she began to stroke the heated skin.

"No… this is wrong."

"As you touching me was wrong?"

He moaned, long and deep. Standing rigid, hands fisted at his sides, eyes closed as he shuddered with every touch of her hand on his flesh. It was like heated steel, Claire thought as she closed her fingers around him and ran them up and down the length.

"Faster—dear Christ, do it faster, Claire," he rasped.

Claire adjusted her position and did as he asked. Leaning forward, she placed a hot kiss on his chest, and he moaned again. Lord, the power of touching him like this was intoxicating. Had he felt the same touching her? She wanted his release almost as much as she'd wanted her own. One of his hands fisted in her hair. Pulling her head back, his mouth crushed hers, and she felt him shudder, his body stiffening beneath her hands.

"God, Claire, I'm sorry." He pulled away from her when he was spent and went behind the screen. Returning with a damp cloth, he then washed her hands.

"I'm not sorry, Simon. It was wonderful."

He threw the cloth aside, then did up the buttons of her nightdress. "I should not have done that… or let you—"

Claire placed her hand over his mouth. "Say nothing more, Simon. What we just did was beautiful, and I won't have you ruin it with apologies. Do you understand?"

He nodded, so she released him and lay back on the bed. Turning on her side, she smiled in the darkness. She felt tired now, as if someone had drained all the blood from her body, it was a wonderful feeling. Claire should be shocked at what they'd done, and yet she wasn't. Perhaps in the clear light of day, that would change, but right now she simply wanted to lay here with Simon and sleep. He soon joined her, she felt him press his front to her back, one arm pulling her tight into his body. They did not speak again and in minutes, both were asleep. Claire with a smile still on her face.

AT DAWN, they were again on the road. This time the journey would end in Liverpool. Simon was relieved to see no discomfort or regret on Claire's face as she looked at him across the coach. He attempted to push visions of what they had shared last night out of his head, but Christ it was not easy. Her passion, and the sensual side of her nature had surprised him. She had wanted more, urged him to do what he had, and then she'd done the same to him. His body stirred at the memory of her hands on him. She'd been responsive, passionate, and Simon feared he'd never want another, as he now did Claire Belmont. Now was not the time to think about this, however. They had to concentrate on the child.

"Do you want to look at the note again, Simon?"

He took it from her, although he knew every word, as he had memorized it the first time he'd read it. He tucked it in his pocket, as he was not sure he would need to show it to whomever held the child. However he wished to be prepared for all eventualities.

"Claire, I must insist you follow my lead on this. These men could be dangerous, and we have no idea what we are stepping into. Plus," he added as she opened her mouth, "I have been into the Anchor once, and it is not a place frequented by respectable people. It is rough, loud, and filled with whores and sailors." He'd hoped to scare her, but instead, she lifted her chin.

"This is my niece or nephew, Simon. A few women of loose morals and hardened sailors will not scare me, I assure you, especially after the fight I witnessed not two nights ago."

"I must have your word that you will let me negotiate for the child, Claire. Otherwise, I shall be forced to tie you up and leave you in the carriage." Simon said calmly, when all he could think of doing was hauling her onto his lap and ravishing her smart mouth.

She didn't gasp or look affronted. The only indication she gave that she was agitated was the rise and fall of her splendid breasts, which he had licked last night.

Focus, Kelkirk, for pity's sake.

"Are you threatening me, Lord Kelkirk?"

"Yes, Miss Belmont, I am."

She huffed out a breath. "Can we not approach this as equals?"

"Of course we can, and I will have the final say in all things." Lord, he wanted to laugh as she glared at him. She was feisty, was his Claire.

"I thought you would wait in the carriage," she said.

"No you didn't."

"I'd hoped you would wait in the carriage, then," she clarified.

"Having been through what we have in the last few days and knowing what you do of me, do you think I would let a beautiful woman I care about, go to a tavern, which I have already explained has disreputable patrons, on her own?"

He could see her brain working furiously to try and outmaneuver him. He loved that about her. She always challenged him and was never happy to simply accept his word.

"I'm not beautiful, Simon, so stop trying to flatter me so I will fall in with your plans."

"You are beautiful, and why are you so sure Anthony's son or daughter will be awaiting our arrival? Have you given thought to the fact that Mathew may be right— that this could be a hoax?"

"It is no hoax, Simon, I'm sure of it. And Eva is an example of a beautiful woman, not I."

"Claire, men hang off your skirts every evening. I have watched them. Why, if you are not beautiful, are they doing that?"

Her answer was to wave her hand, which, he guessed, meant she was through discussing the matter.

"I have made it a hobby of mine over the years to observe women, especially beautiful ones." Ignoring her scoffing, he added, "And you are... beautiful, that is."

"I am aware of your extensive study, Simon. Now enough of this silly conversation if you please, as it matters not to me. I would rather we organize what is to be done when we arrive at our destination. How shall we know whom to ask for at the Anchor?"

"It matters to me that you do not see yourself as others do, Claire. It matters very much."

She looked surprised. "Well, thank you, Simon... really."

Clearly, she didn't believe him. It shocked him that she did not realize how beautiful she was. He'd always believed her self-confident and aware of the effect she had on men, but it seemed he was wrong. Miss Claire Belmont was a mass of contradictions and uncertainties, and he'd gotten to know a few of them, but he was sure she was hiding several more.

"We will stop for food now, Claire, as we left without eating, and then press on to Liverpool."

"Mathew is like you. He can't do anything if his stomach is not full."

"We are bigger than you. Therefore we need more food," he added simply. "Plus, my coachmen will be hungry, and whilst you now have their undying devotion, I have to still work at it. Food is always a good bribe."

"Why do I have their undying devotion?" she questioned, frowning.

"Because you walked into a room filled with men who were all engaged in beating each other senseless, stood on a table, and threatened to shoot one of them between his legs."

She rolled her eyes. "Men are silly creatures, to give their devotions so easily."

"So not only do you believe you are not beautiful, but also unworthy of devotion."

She didn't answer, just gave him another look that told him this line of conversation, too, was over. So he started another. This one she would like even less than the last. "Your brother told me at the Waverly musical evening that he had not had much to do with you growing up, Claire, and that he was very sorry about that fact."

She looked away from him and out the window.

"You dreamt about him last night, and your words told me the distance between you is painful. Have you ever talked to Mathew about how you feel, Claire?"

"My brother and I have never been close, and perhaps I am in part to blame. Anthony and I were closer in age, so we spent most of our time together after father passed. And Mathew was forced into the role of Marquis at a young age. I'm sorry now that I did not support him more. It was just that he seemed so capable, and I did not think he needed me. However, it is too late now. After this, the distance between us will be insurmountable."

He remembered the words she'd spoken in her sleep, her need for someone to comfort her when she was alone at night.

"You more than anyone know about living behind a façade, Claire. Did you not credit your brother with the same pretense as you?"

"It seems I should have, but now I fear it is too late to attempt to change what lies between us."

Simon took her hands in his. "It's never too late."

She gave a sad little laugh. "Not all men talk like you, Simon, and Mathew is like me. We don't share our feelings easily. I fear after this there will be an even greater divide between us."

"You don't know that. When he is presented with his niece or nephew, he may forgive you everything."

"I am doing nothing wrong, Simon. It is I who will need to forgive him first."

She was right, of course. If there was a niece or nephew awaiting them in Liverpool, then Mathew Belmont would have much to forgive himself for.

"You said your parents were not loving, Simon, but were they fair?"

He hadn't expected that turn in conversation and had no time to school his features, so instead, he turned away from her. "Why do you want to know?" He knew he sounded defensive yet he had no desire to discuss his past.

"You were an only child?" She said ignoring his question for one of her own.

Simon had buried the years with his parents deep inside him. Not because it still hurt him—it was just something he had now put aside, as after his parents' deaths, his life had really begun. Only then had he known it was possible to live with two people and know happiness.

"I am," he said adding nothing further. Luckily the carriage chose that moment to stop. Relieved, Simon ignored the curiosity in her eyes and reached for the door. "I will get us some food." He had the door open before she could protest and was back within minutes with a plate of freshly baked scones. After giving Ben and Merlin some, he then rejoined Claire in the carriage.

"Ben and Merlin think very highly of you, Simon."

Simon was relieved that Claire seemed to have dropped her earlier line of questioning. He took a large bite of his scone before answering, enjoying the warm, doughy mixture in his mouth. "I treat them fairly—that is all, Claire. Now you need to eat something."

"I don't really think I could eat now." She eyed the offerings with wariness, as if they were not fresh and slathered with jam and heavenly tasting.

"Be sensible, Claire. You need to keep up your strength for what is to come."

"You have a lot in common with my brother when you talk like that." She took the scone reluctantly and nibbled like a rabbit on the edge.

"I begin to sympathize with him," Simon muttered, eating one scone in three bites before reaching for another.

"At least chew before you swallow," she said.

"Shrew."

"Heathen."

He returned her smile and felt something flow between them. He wasn't sure what, but it left him feeling ridiculously happy, which, in the normal course of his life, would have terrified him spitless. However, surprisingly, it now left him feeling warm right to his toes.

. . .

Claire could barely sit still as the carriage approached the outskirts of Liverpool. The scene was not sitting well, and she felt sick at the prospect of the upcoming encounter. Across from her, Simon sat calmly, gazing, for the most, out the window. Occasionally he would look at her, and she knew it was to check that she was all right. The bruise on his chin was now a dark shade of plum, and his eye was black. If not dressed like a gentleman, he could be mistaken for someone with more nefarious intentions.

When the first ship's mast came into view, she wanted to tell him to turn the carriage around, that this had been a mistake. But of course, she could not, not when a child relied on her—Anthony's child, she reminded herself.

"Take a deep breath, Claire." Simon had a gentle look on his face as he held out a hand to her. She clutched it and drew in a shuddering lung full of air. "And another, sweetheart. That's it."

How had she come to rely on this man? He was so much more than she'd believed him to be, or had allowed herself to see. How had she been foolish enough to run away from him, believing she could do this on her own? "Thank you, Simon."

"You're welcome, Claire." He went back to looking out the window, but her fingers remained in his.

"I'm scared." The words had left her mouth before she could swallow them down. It seemed that now she had told him so much about herself, she was unable to hold anything back.

"I would be foolish to tell you not to be, Claire, yet I would ask you to trust me to keep both you and the child safe."

"I do trust you, Simon, and these past few days have only strengthened that trust, but my fears are not just for myself and the child. My fears are for you, also."

"Thank you, but I'm sure your fears are unfounded. We

could walk into that tavern and collect the child and be out of there in ten minutes."

"But that's highly unlikely, don't you think?"

"Unlikely but possible," he added firmly.

"Promise me you will not fight anyone, Simon."

His laughter rolled around the carriage. "You make it sound as if I had a choice the other night, Claire. I had no option but to fight. Had I not, they would have attacked me, anyway, and as I was not about to flee—"

"You should have fled."

"Now, there, I'm afraid, you are asking too much of me." He looked like a rogue with all those bruises on his face—a very handsome rogue.

"I will never understand men."

"We are really quite simple, my sweet, unlike members of your fair sex, who have more sides than Lady Pepper's corset. We look after what's ours, fill our bellies, and like to show our strength upon occasion."

Claire didn't want to think about another woman belonging to him, so instead, she said what she had been rehearsing for the past few miles. "Simon, should something go wrong and we are seen by someone we know, then you are not to take responsibility, nor will you do anything drastic like offer marriage to save my reputation. I went into this with my eyes open, just as—" *Lord, this is hard.* "Just as what we did last night does not make you bound to me. I alone will take responsibility for any consequences as a result of my actions."

She had been the recipient of that steady look many times on this journey.

"A very pretty speech I am sure, but if you think that what happened on this journey and last night hasn't changed everything between us, then you are fooling only yourself, Claire. Furthermore I am involved, and aware of the consequence should someone see us, and I will face those responsibilities should they arise."

"No, Simon, please— Dear lord, we are here." Every other thought slipped Claire's head as the carriage slowed. She gripped Simon's fingers hard.

"Take another breath, Claire, before you run out of air."

"Of c-course." She had not realized how quickly she was breathing. Inhaling, she released the breath slowly.

"Now here is what we will do, and I want you to listen carefully and make sure you do what I tell you."

She nodded because she was sure if she spoke, her teeth would chatter.

"I will go into the Anchor first and ascertain if it is safe for you to enter."

"Oh but—"

"No buts, Claire, you will do exactly as I say."

CHAPTER THIRTEEN

Simon stopped her from saying anything further by placing his hand over her mouth. "I will make a few discreet inquiries, and then, when I have the identity of the man we need to speak with, I shall come and collect you. Women like you are not seen in places like the Anchor, Claire, so we need to make sure you are in there no longer than necessary."

She nodded, so he lowered his hand, yet the warm imprint of her mouth remained on his palm. "I understand."

"No you don't, or at least, you don't want to. Yet you will do this Claire, as it is for your safety as well as mine."

"I don't want you to put yourself in danger, Simon." Her small fingers wrapped around his wrist as she leant forward. Her brown eyes searched his desperately.

"I won't, and I have told you it is my choice to be here. Now be a good girl and keep out of sight."

She surprised him by placing her lips on his. The taste of her instantly filled his head, bringing back memories of her beneath him. Taking her shoulders, he pulled her closer, deepening the kiss. She didn't pull away. Instead, wrapping her arms around his shoulders and holding him close. He'd never wanted a woman the way he did Claire. She made his body burn with need, and he feared it was a fire that would never be extinguished.

"Be careful, Simon," she whispered when he released her. Her lips looked red and swollen, and something primitive inside him reveled in the knowledge that he had marked her.

"I will, and I promise to return to you soon."

Simon spoke to his drivers before he made for the Anchor. "Miss Belmont is not to leave the carriage until I return, Merlin, no matter how persuasive she becomes. Is that understood?"

"Yes, my lord."

He made his way down the street toward the Anchor. The port was busy. There were noises and people everywhere. Rigging clanged, vendors hawked their wares, and children darted across the street between rolling barrels, carts and adults. It did not take him long to reach the Anchor. Once there he pushed open the door and walked inside.

The scent of ale and dried sweat greeted him as he entered the dark interior. The walls were covered with various items from ships, and the men inside were mostly sailors. Several ladies who were offering more than ale to the patrons walked among the men, displaying as much of their bodies as they could without removing their clothing. Simon made his way to the bar, where he bought an ale and looked around the room. He discounted most of the men he saw as people just biding their time before ships left the port, and then his eyes fell on a seaman sitting at the rear of the room. Taking a sip of his ale, Simon watched the man motion the woman who approached him away. He had no drink in front of him, and to Simon's eye, he looked as if he was waiting for someone.

Removing a handful of coins from inside his pocket, he motioned the bartender closer.

"Looks like you've run into a handful of trouble by that face."

Simon's smile was feral. "Indeed, but the other man looks worse than me, it pleases me to say."

The bartender ran his eyes over Simon, taking in the fine clothes, but said nothing further.

"The seaman sitting at the table in the rear—has he been here before?" he questioned, placing the coins on the bar.

"Every day at the same time for a week. Tight-fisted French sod, never orders a bleeding drink—just keeps his eyes on the door for a while, then leaves." Pocketing the coins, the bartender left to serve another customer.

Drink in hand, Simon made his way toward the man. Once there, he pulled out the chair opposite and sat.

"I am waiting for someone, sir. Please leave."

He wasn't tall. However, his shoulders were muscled and his forearms beefy. His English was broken, so Simon answered him in French.

"I would never have allowed my sister to travel here alone, sir, so you will deal with me or not at all."

"Lord Belmont?" The man's eyes gave Simon a calculating look.

"And you are?"

"Never mind who I am, only that I have something your family wants."

Simon sat back in his chair and took a sip from his drink, trying not to wince. He would have preferred tea or coffee at this hour, and the glass had a salty taste to the lip that was not pleasant.

"Why did you lure my sister into that lane?"

"We had the boy in London and had hoped to hand him to her before coming here to catch our ship."

He was telling the truth, Simon thought. Still, he had to take precautions. "And how do I know you are not just trying to extort money from me? After all, there is obviously no child nearby."

The man's eyes darted around the room and then back to Simon. "My sister gave this to me on her deathbed. It's a note from your brother, stating that if he did not return for her, then something must have happened, and if she ever needed help, she was to contact your sister."

Simon took the note and read the contents. He had no idea if this was Anthony's handwriting or not. Claire would know, however. Handing it back, Simon said, "So you are selling your sister's child, now she has died? It warms my heart, sir, to see such family loyalty."

The man's fists clenched on the table at Simon's taunt.

"My brother and I have no place in our lives for a child!"

"So you are prepared to abandon it?" The man had the grace to lower his head, but he said nothing further.

Simon heard the voices around them grow quiet and knew with a sinking feeling that Claire had entered the tavern.

"Your sister has arrived, my lord."

"So it would seem," Simon said, standing. "And I'm going to kill her," he added softly as he caught her eyes. "Excuse me. I shall return shortly."

She was standing beside Merlin, who, in turn, was looking at Simon with a desperate expression on his face. Men were closing in on her, but whatever expression was on Simon's face was sending them away without a word. "You promised me, Claire."

"You did not return, and I grew worried." His anger did not seem to scare her, as it did the men.

"God, woman, you would try the patience of a saint," Simon hissed, taking her arm and hauling her into his side, thereby declaring she belonged to him. "And you were given orders not to let her leave the carriage, Merlin," he added, turning on his driver.

"It is not his fault, Simon. I told him I needed to have some privacy, if you know what I mean."

"She was right convincing, my lord. Ben held the horses whilst I accompanied her, and then she picked up her skirts and ran across the street toward the Anchor."

Merlin should have been outraged by Claire's actions. Instead, Simon could see only admiration. Resigned, Simon looked down at the woman at his side. "Why am I not surprised?"

"Is the man you were talking to the one, Simon?"

"Yes, and he believes I am your brother, so play along. In his possession is a letter he states is from Anthony. You will ask to look it over and then confirm it is your brother's handwriting. Merlin, stand at our rear whilst Miss Belmont and I go and talk to the man." His driver mumbled his agreement, and they made their way back across the room.

"This is my sister, Miss Belmont. Claire, this man has not furnished me with his name." She sat in the seat Simon held out for her.

"My brother has informed me you have a letter from Anthony, sir. I wish to see it, if you please." The hand she held out shook slightly and then steadied as she began to read. Simon watched as her eyes followed each word. She then folded it precisely and handed it back to the man. "Your sister obviously meant a great deal to my brother if he wrote that note for her."

Claire's confirmation of the authenticity of the letter told Simon that if there was a child, then it was possibly Anthony's.

"My sister gave her favors too freely," the man growled and then spat out a foul curse.

"I would ask you to watch the way you speak in front of my sister, sir. Our brother meant a great deal to us, and I will not have his name blackened."

He was not foolish enough to antagonize Simon further, so he clamped his mouth into a grim line.

"Now as I'm sure you will not just hand the child over without payment, how much do you want?"

The seaman's eyes darted from Claire to Simon before he spoke. "My brother and I want money for our future, and in case we get hurt and can't sail no more."

"How much?" Simon put his hand over Claire's as her fingers clenched. The man told him an amount that was high but not excessively so. "I will not give you a penny until I see the child." He squeezed the hand beneath his as it tensed.

"I want half now."

Simon stared at the man silently for several seconds and hoped Claire would hold her tongue, too. "Not a penny until I see the child, and then you will have it all."

"I want half now."

"Then we have nothing further to say to each other." Simon said, regaining his feet and lifting Claire from her chair.

"Simon." He could hear the desperation in that single word, but he held strong.

"Trust me," he whispered, propelling her forward. They made it to the doorway before his voice reached them.

"All right, I shall bring the child here in one hour. We will meet down by the Bonny Rose."

Simon simply nodded and walked Claire through the doorway, with Merlin now at their heels.

"It's all right," he soothed, placing an arm around her waist. "It will be over soon."

"Do you think Anthony cared for that woman and that is why he left her the note, Simon?"

All around them, noise sounded, people brushed by, but he was as focused on her as she was on him. "I'm sure he did, Claire."

Simon saw a tearoom, and, ushering her inside, he motioned for Merlin to come, too, and then ordered food and drinks. Simon watched her as they ate. She did not speak, and her eyes kept looking to the tall masts in the distance. As the minutes ticked by, her pallor increased.

"Simon, what if the child is not Anthony's?"

"You've just endured possibly the most trying three days of your life during which you've told me constantly that it is, and the note confirmed your brother knew the woman, so why, suddenly, do you think it isn't?"

Her eyes were shadowed with uncertainty. "Doubts are suddenly plaguing me, now the time draws near. Am I doing the right thing? How will I know if the child is Anthony's? Doubts that I have embroiled you in this, and it may all be for naught."

"I've told you repeatedly that it was my choice to accompany you, Claire. And it's my belief you will know if the child is of your blood when you see it."

"If someone sees us or hears of the time we spent alone, I will be ruined and your name will be blackened, Simon. Please, dear lord, let my niece or nephew be waiting for me so I may confirm, if only to us, that what I have done is the right thing."

"Don't lose your courage now, Claire—not when it has carried you so far. I admired your strength before this journey, and my admiration has increased tenfold since."

She managed a small smile, and then fell silent again. He looked at his watch and caught his coachman's eye. "Merlin, now you've finished eating every crumb on the plates, I would like you to bring the carriage as close to the ship named The Bonny Rose as you possibly can."

"At once, my lord."

"It is time for us to leave now, Claire."

Simon watched as she opened her reticule and handed him a purse. "This is for payment, Simon. It is not quite enough, as I had to use some—"

"To flee from me in the middle of the night," Simon said.

She gave one abrupt nod before continuing. "So if you could see your way to paying the rest, I will repay you when I return to London."

Simon took the bag and counted the money, adding some of his own before closing it. He then stood and held out his hand. She clutched it, and together they walked down to the ship. He was getting used to the feel of her hand in his.

They heard gulls, and the tang of the sea air surrounded them as they strolled down to the ship. Other people passed, and Simon doffed his hat while Claire forced a smile onto her face, and then the ship was before them, tall masts rolling gently from side to side.

"Do you see him, Claire?"

She followed his gaze and then came to a sudden halt as her eyes fell on the small child standing beside the man they had met in the Anchor.

"Oh lord, he has Anthony's hair, Simon, almost the same color as mine." She started walking again. However, now she was dragging him. Her strides were long and hurried as she closed the distance in seconds. The man saw them coming and bent to whisper something in the boy's ear. The child, in turn, moved away to stand with two men at the foot of the gangway leading up to the Bonny Rose.

"You have seen the child. Now hand over the money."

"I want the letter, too," Simon said, holding out the pouch. The man pulled the letter out of his pocket and passed it to him. He counted the money and then signaled for the boy to be brought forward.

"This is your aunt and uncle, Louis. You will be going with them now."

Another man placed a small bag at the boy's feet, and then they all left without another word, climbing the gangway. There was no hug or brief word or pat on the head from the boy's real uncle. The man had left his nephew alone with two strangers without a backward glance.

THE BREATH CAUGHT in Claire's throat as Louis looked up at her. It was her brother's face and brown eyes that stared back at her. Fighting tears, she dropped to her knees before him and smiled. Dear lord, if she had not come, what would have happened to this child? Her heart ached for him as he waited silently to find out what his fate would be. Claire did not know many children, yet the ones she did know were continually moving, talking, or crying. This one, however, was solemn and still. Tentatively, she took one of his small hands in hers. He didn't flinch, which she hoped was a sign that he had not been mistreated.

"I understand you are scared, Louis."

"He will only speak French, Claire."

She gave Simon a grateful smile before continuing this time in French. "I understand you don't know me or this man beside me whose name is Simon, yet I want you to know we will never hurt you. I am your aunt, Louis, and I want to care for you, if you will let me."

He didn't move, just studied her with that emotionless expression. He had not been starved, as he was healthy enough to the eye, nor were his clothes ragged. However he needed both a wash and a comb, as he smelt of fish and his hair was matted. She wondered who, besides his mother, had hugged him and kissed his soft little cheeks. Had anyone wiped his tears when he cried or sat him on their laps?

Simon lowered himself to his haunches beside her. "Hello, Louis. Are you hungry?"

Claire smiled as the little boy nodded. Simon knew the exact thing to say to make him respond. It was a trait of his, the ability to weigh a tricky situation and then take the measures necessary to resolve it.

"Come, then, and we shall fill that little belly of yours."

She held her breath as Simon reached for the boy, his hands lifting him high to settle Louis against his shoulder. Standing, he turned to her.

"Come on, Aunty Claire. Louis and I are hungry."

Hurrying to her feet, she took the hand Simon held out to her. She had never really liked to be touched, and yet now she liked it very much. Well, what she actually liked was Simon's touch. Picking up Louis's bag, she let him and Simon lead her back up the hill to the carriage. As they arrived, she turned for one last look at the ship that had brought her nephew to her, and it was then her eyes fell on the couple walking toward them. "No!"

Simon turned to see what had disturbed her and then cursed softly. She watched him quickly place Louis in the carriage. "Louis, please wait in the carriage while your aunt and I purchase you some food."

Relieved, Claire watched as the boy climbed onto a seat, eyes wide as he looked around the elegant interior. Simon then closed the door before turning to face the couple heading their way. "Smile, Claire, and walk with me away from the carriage. Slowly," he cautioned her as she began to hurry.

"Lord Kelkirk, Miss Belmont, this is a surprise."

Claire tried to look pleased to see the couple now before her when she was anything but. The Countess of Tinley was a gossip, and by the look in her eye, she knew she was about to get a juicy tidbit.

"What has happened to your face, my lord?"

"An altercation with a pickpocket, I'm afraid. However, no lasting damage has been done."

"You must tell me what has you both here… alone?" the countess cooed.

"Good morning, Lord Tinley," Simon said, ignoring the countess's question to acknowledge her husband.

"Kelkirk."

"My lord, I must insist you tell me what has you both here in Liverpool alone?"

"We are not alone, Countess. Miss Belmont's maid is accompanying my aunt while she looks in some of the shops," he said waving a hand to the left where the shops were. "Miss Belmont and I are taking a walk before collecting her and continuing on our journey."

"Your, aunt!" The countess declared clapping her hands together. "It has been so long since I saw her."

"I'm sorry but we are in a hurry, Countess, therefore we must be on our way. However she and my uncle will be visiting me in London soon. Perhaps you could call on her then."

Anyone listening to Simon would think he was discussing the weather, he sounded unruffled and composed. However it would take more than he to deter the countess when she believed there was a titillating story to be had, Claire thought with a sinking feeling. He was lying to a woman who cut her eye teeth on gossip. The countess liked to know everything about everyone and she would question them until she had the answers she desired, and if they were not forthcoming, she would simply make them up.

"But to leave so early in the season, Lord Kelkirk… where is it you and Miss Belmont travel with your aunt?"

"And you, Countess? What has you here in Liverpool?"

Claire watched the woman's eyes narrow as Simon deflected the question.

"We are visiting with Captain Withers as we do every year at this time, my lord."

The silence that followed made Claire's toes curl inside her shoes.

"I'm sure I overheard your mother saying you were visiting with the Duke and Duchess of Stratton at their estate, Miss Belmont."

"We had a change of plans," Simon said calmly.

"We?" The countess cooed. "I had not realized you were such friends, my lord."

This was bad, bad, bad. Claire felt the water close over her head as she struggled to come up with an excuse for why she was here with Simon.

"It seems our secret is out, darling."

Shocked, Claire looked up at Simon, who, in turn, was smiling down at her. However the gesture did not reach his eyes.

"Simon, no—"

"Secret, Lord Kelkirk?"

"Miss Belmont has consented to be my wife, and we are on our way back to London after visiting with my aunt and uncle, Countess. I would ask that you keep our little surprise for a few days, if you could."

Claire couldn't speak. Her tongue seemed to have swollen, and her limbs felt suddenly heavy. Dear god, what was Simon thinking? She had to put a stop to it before the countess had a chance to tell anyone. "No, really, Lady Tinley—"

"It's all right, darling. We can rely on the earl and countess to keep our secret." His tone was light, yet there was nothing gentle about the fingers that dug into her waist.

"Congratulations, Kelkirk!" the earl boomed.

"And the dear little child I saw with you, my lord? To whom does he belong?"

"He is my driver's child, Countess." Simon said, looking at Merlin who was seated on the carriage behind him. "I let him come along when his father is going on long journeys, as his mother passed a few months ago."

More guilt piled onto Claire's shoulders as Simon invented another lie on her behalf.

"That is very sweet of you, my lord," the countess said believing his every word. "But now we must away. Come, husband, we will leave the lovebirds to their journey. Congratulations to you both," the countess gushed, kissing Claire's cheek.

"Of course your secret is safe with us."

Like hell it was.

She watched the elderly couple leave before turning to face the man at her side. "Dear god, Simon, what have you done?"

The hand on her back fell away. "And what would you have me say? That you are here to collect your dead brother's illegitimate child and that you spent three nights in my arms, one of them doing things only a married woman should? Damn it, Claire, you have no maid or companion with you, had that woman decided to pursue the matter then she would have found that out. What else could I say?"

"Yes, I know you did what you did, to protect me. Forgive me, I should not have spoken that way," Claire attempted to calm down. "But I won't let this happen, Simon. I promise to find a way out of this mess I've created."

"Too late. Now get into the carriage before your nephew gets frightened over our absence." His voice was cold and emotionless and the fingers on her wrist hard.

"No, Simon, I won't let this happen." She tried to get him

to release her, but he just kept on walking and towing her with him.

"It's done. Now be quiet and get in the carriage."

"Don't tell me to be quiet," Claire said as calmly as she could. She was horrified at what he had just done, especially as he had done it to save her. "I have every right to talk to you about this. You have no wish to marry me, just as I have no wish to marry you."

He stopped suddenly, spinning her around to face him. "What would you have had me do, Miss Belmont? It was not only your reputation at stake."

"You should have blamed me. I told you I would probably be retiring from society, anyway. Now it is going to be so much worse. My family will hear about this before I have a chance to clear things up."

"And that would have been a gentlemanly thing to do in your eyes would it? Leave you to face censure and yes, disgrace, alone. While I stood quietly to one side and let you?"

"No, but it would have been the right course of action to take, Simon. We discussed this—"

"You discussed it, and I listened without comment. Now be quiet. I have told the earl and countess we are to marry, so we will."

She had rarely seen that look on Simon's face. It was closed and emotionless. There was none of the softness she had come to know so well. His eyes were so cold now, as they looked down at her. He would do this because he was an honorable man, but Claire would not let him. "We could never marry. You would not be happy, nor would I."

The hands on her arms tightened briefly, and then he released her. "It's done and there is one area in which we are compatible. The rest will follow."

"You're being deliberately vulgar."

"I'm being honest. Believe me, it is a lot more than many marriages start with. Now get in the carriage." And that, it seemed, was his final word, because he opened the door and bundled her inside.

Louis was huddled in the corner when they entered. He looked at their hands and noticed they were empty and frowned.

"I promise to get your food soon, Louis—have patience," Simon stated, patting the boy's head. The child nodded and then watched Claire take the seat opposite him.

"I will fix this, Simon. I promise," she said slowly.

"Let it be, Claire." He sounded so tired suddenly, as if the last few minutes had aged him, and the effort of talking was too great. She had done this to him— stepped into his well-ordered life and disrupted it, and only she could change it back. She had to, or she would never be able to live with the consequences.

"I'm so sorry, Simon."

One big hand rested briefly over hers, and then he knocked on the roof, and soon the carriage was on its way. After getting Louis his food, they traveled until it was dark. The boy slept for a while, his head resting in Claire's lap, but woke when they stopped at another inn for the night. Simon explained to the proprietor that they were a family and needed lodgings. A supper was brought to their rooms, and after they washed their faces and hands, Simon told her he would see to Merlin and Ben and that she and Louis should sleep on the bed whilst he slept on the floor. Before she could reply, he left the room. With a heavy heart, Claire found Louis's nightshirt and helped him into it. She then tucked him into bed and sat down beside him.

"Will you sleep now, Louis?" Claire said in French.

"Oui."

His eyes looked at her, solemn and expressionless, yet she

knew he must be scared. How could she soothe those fears? He had been wrenched from everything he had known in his short life—taken to England and left with strangers. Claire could not begin to comprehend how he must feel. "Did you know, Louis, that your papa was my brother?"

He shook his head, but his eyes remained on hers. "He was the very best of men, and he would have loved you very much." She pushed the hair back from his forehead. "And you look so much like him. It is as if he is here with me now."

Claire talked to Louis of Anthony and her family—now his family, she hoped— until his eyes grew heavy, and finally, he slept. He was so small and vulnerable lying in the big bed, and she felt the weight of responsibility upon her. She was all he had now, especially if her brother did not back down from the stand he had taken. She rubbed her chest in a futile attempt to ease the ache inside. He was hers to love, and love him she would, for as long as he needed her.

Leaving the bed, Claire then changed into her nightdress and lay down beside him. She left the candle burning for Simon and closed her eyes to rest. There would be no sleep, not with her thoughts so full. She had Louis to think of now, and she also needed to figure out a way to break her engagement to Simon without his reputation being harmed.

She heard Simon enter but kept her eyes closed. He removed his boots, as she heard one hit the floor, and then his clothing. She imagined him down to his breeches and remembered the wonderful feelings he had created in her last night. She could feel his hard, pulsing flesh beneath her hands as she'd stroked him and hear his hoarse cries as he'd found his release. Last night, they had been lovers, tonight they were strangers.

She felt the brief brush of his fingers on the back of her hand, and opened her eyes to find him above her.

"Rest, Claire, everything will be all right.

"I'm so sorry Simon," she whispered. He didn't answer and she heard him settle on the floor, and in minutes the sound of his deep regular breathing told her he was asleep. Staring into the darkness, Claire was surprised to find her own eyes growing heavy. Her last thought was, that she would do what needed to be done to make things right again between them.

CHAPTER FOURTEEN

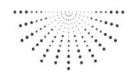

By the third day, Louis had realized neither Claire nor Simon meant him any harm and had relaxed enough to talk a little. He had no brothers or sisters, and his mother had been an angel, and he missed the town he came from because there, he could fish every day.

"But you can fish here, too, Louis," Simon said, his face softening when he addressed the child. With Claire, he was polite, yet there was now a distance between them and she missed him. She yearned for his arms around her, but most of all, she wanted her friend to return, the one who challenged her and made her laugh. She tried to talk to him, raise the subject of what was to be done, but he just shook his head and told her they would talk later, however they were to marry and she needed to accept that.

"We are stopping for the night at my estate, Claire, and tomorrow we will reach London, as it is a short drive."

"Will your aunt and uncle be present?"

He nodded and then turned away to say something to Louis, and that, she guessed, was the end to the conversation.

The light was fading as they drove up the drive to Simon's

estate. Claire could still see how vast it was, the grass edging the narrow roadway seemed to roll for many miles. Then the horses clattered over a stone bridge and swept into a circular driveway.

"What will we tell them about Louis, Simon? Your aunt and uncle will need to know why he is with us and why I am alone with you."

He looked at her briefly. "My aunt and uncle do not go out in society, Claire. Therefore, we will tell them the truth."

"I don't think we—"

"I have never lied to them. I will not I start now."

Claire placed her hand on his arm as he prepared to open the carriage. "I am merely trying to protect Louis, Simon. There will be enough people throughout his life willing to hurt him. I have no wish for it to start now."

"They are good people, Claire. You have my word he will be safe here."

She followed him from the carriage, and then held out her arms to Louis and was surprised when he went into them willingly. She often had this warm feeling inside her when she held Georgia, now she had Louis, she would have it more, as it would be she who cared for him from this day forward.

"You are safe here with me and Simon, Louis," she whispered as his two thin arms wrapped about her neck.

"Come," Simon said, waving for her to follow him. She missed the feel of his hand wrapped around hers, but one look at his closed expression told her that was not likely to happen ever again.

She found strength in the small body in her arms as they walked up the stairs and into the huge entranceway.

"Good evening, Lord Kelkirk."

"Good evening, Morgan. I fear we are about to trouble

you and the staff. You see, I need three rooms prepared, with baths and meals, please."

"No trouble at all, my lord."

The floors were polished marble and the stairs huge and sweeping with banisters that shone. Paintings hung on the walls and statues stood in alcoves. It was the home of a man with substantial wealth, and whilst she had known Simon's was a comfortable fortune, she had not known just how comfortable.

"Where are my aunt and uncle, Morgan?"

"In the conservatory, my lord." "Is he too heavy, Claire?"

Shaking her head in answer to Simon's query, Claire followed him down a long hallway that branched to the left beneath the staircase. She saw more paintings and a glass-fronted cabinet filled with pretty little knickknacks before they reached a door Simon opened. After descending several steps, they arrived in the conservatory.

Tall, leafy plants and bright blooms filled the room, and the combined scents were wonderful. They walked down a white stone path, and Louis lifted his head from Claire's shoulder, as he heard the sound of water coming from a small indoor fountain up ahead. His eyes, like hers, moved from left to right as they studied each new sight. She wanted to ask Simon questions but was too nervous to do so. Claire heard the sound of voices and then saw two people sitting in comfortable chairs with a tray of tea on the table before them. At their backs, the soft sunlight of early evening streamed through the big windows.

The woman was dressed elegantly in a high-necked emerald gown. Her grey hair was pulled into a soft knot on top of her head. The man, too, was dressed immaculately and it was he who saw them first.

"Simon!"

The delight on their faces as they saw their nephew was

genuine and quickly changed to concern when they saw his bruises. Claire stood back as Simon greeted his family. She heard his deep voice speaking softly for several minutes and then felt the eyes of his uncle and aunt upon her. What were they thinking? Simon had said they were good people, yet surely they would be shocked over her behavior, and the fact that their nephew had gained his injuries because of her.

As if sensing her tension, Louis tightened his arms around her neck. "I have you," Claire whispered, hugging him close.

"Miss Belmont, please come and sit down. You must be tired." Simon's aunt walked forward, holding out her hands to Claire. "And this is Louis, I believe. Hello, young man."

Claire sat and turned Louis in her arms so he could look at the other people.

"You may relax here, dear. Simon's friends will always be safe and welcome in our home. We understand you have had quite an adventure and now must return to London to face your family."

She sent Simon a brief look. Had he told them of the betrothal?

"Yes, it has been a difficult time," Claire said, feeling her way. "I would like to thank you very much for opening your home to me and Louis and on such short acquaintance, especially considering the circumstances."

"This is Simon's home, my dear. We merely look after it for him."

Of course she'd known that but wasn't sure what to say.

"It is your home as much as mine, aunt, as I have told you both many times." Simon's words made his elderly relations smile, and he smiled in return. A soft, gentle smile, the kind that until Liverpool, he had bestowed on her.

More tea was brought, and Simon talked with his family, who, in turn, tried to coax her into conversation. Claire was good at social chatter, yet the art seemed to be failing her now.

"And how is the season going for you, my dear?"

"Uh... I very well, thank you."

"Do you like fish, Louis?" Simon's uncle asked the boy, who nodded. "Well then, come with me, and I will show you something."

Claire watched in surprise as her nephew climbed off her lap, took the man's hand, and allowed him to lead him deeper into the conservatory.

"If you will excuse me, there are things that need my attention." Simon rose and gave them a bow without meeting Claire's eyes, and then he, too, was gone.

"He is preoccupied, Claire, but it is not with you that he is angry. It is for the circumstances that were thrust upon you." Claire saw no censure in the woman's eyes.

"Yes, he has much on his mind, and I'm afraid I have contributed to his concerns."

"I understand that Louis is your late brother's child?"

Claire nodded, unsure how much Simon had said.

"And that you must return to London tomorrow to tell your family of his existence?"

Not true, strictly speaking, as her family already knew about Louis. However she would have to tell Mathew that she had defied him and now had Louis in her care. Nodding again, Claire said yes, that was the case.

"It will not be an easy interview, from what I gather, and I would like to offer to look after Louis for you here until you return."

"Oh no, I could not impose. Nor would I like Louis to think I have abandoned him so soon."

Eyes like Simon's offered her a soft smile. "My husband and I have a great deal of experience with wounded young boys, Claire, and we will ensure he is both safe and happy until you are in a position to return for him."

"I could not impose upon you like that."

Her smile was genuine. "It would be no imposition. In fact, we would be glad of the company."

"How much did Simon tell you about my situation?"

"That you now have your nephew in your care and need to inform your family of that fact, and no more."

She was not lying. Claire could see the honesty. At least he had not mentioned what he had been forced to do in Liverpool.

"If Louis is happy with that arrangement, then I would be grateful, as it will not be for long. I will return in a few days, and we will retire to my brother's estate." *Hopefully*, Claire added silently. She hoped Mathew did not turn his back on her and Louis entirely.

"And now you must be exhausted, so I shall show you to your room."

"Would it be too much of an imposition to show Louis and I around your gardens? I believe it is a passion to all of you." Claire didn't want to go to her room and rest. She wanted to see Simon's home because she knew this would very possibly be her only chance.

"Are you sure, my dear?"

"Yes, please."

"My name is Penelope, Claire, and my husband is Peter."

She had just only arrived here, but Claire knew deep in her heart that like their nephew, these were very good people. Regaining her feet, she took Penelope's hand and squeezed it gently. The paper-thin skin felt fragile against her fingers, yet Claire thought that perhaps in Penelope's case, appearances could be deceiving and that Simon's aunt had a great deal of strength.

They collected Louis and Peter and opened the glass

doors and walked outside into the warm evening. Claire had visited many country homes in her lifetime for house parties or to visit friends of her mother's, yet none had touched her like this one. This was a home with a heart. She knew the extensive gardens had been planted with love and tended with care, and she was sure Simon's hands had played their part.

"Through there are the glasshouses, Claire," Peter said, pointing beyond a neatly trimmed hedge. "It would be of no interest to a small boy, so Penelope and I will take Louis to see the lake."

"Yes, do go, Claire. The smell is beautiful."

Peter held out his hand to Louis, who took it without hesitation.

"All right. I shall look and then come and join you."

Claire walked, enjoying the silence and the now cooling air. She needed to think, but she knew there would be plenty of time during the long night ahead of her to do so. For now, she would enjoy the quiet and the beauty around her. She found a gap in the hedge and slipped through. Two large glasshouses stood a short distance away. She headed for the first, and finding the door, she entered.

The smell was different in here. There was a dampness in the air, and the scents a mixture of things. A noise came from up ahead, a muttering that indicated she was not alone. Heart thumping, she drew closer, knowing it would be Simon.

He stood with both hands pushed deep in the potted soil on the opposite side of a tall, narrow table. Head bent, he was inspecting a small green plant.

"Simon, I'm sorry, but your aunt told me to come here. She said I would like to see inside the glasshouses." The words rushed from Claire's mouth. "I have no wish to intrude, so I will leave at once."

He didn't move, just lifted his head and gave her a long,

cool look before speaking. "When I have a lot on my mind, I do this."

She walked to the other side of the table. "Put your hands in soil?"

"It calms me, somehow. The feel of the earth sifting through my fingers gives me clarity."

Claire slowly pulled off her gloves. "Did you often need to feel calm, Simon?"

He expelled a breath through his teeth at her question.

Claire located a sturdy box and dragged it closer.

"What are you doing?" he questioned as she stood on it.

"Joining you." Pushing her hands into the earth, her fingers touched the tips of his briefly before she curled them into fists and broke the contact. He watched her as she played with the earth—sifted it, patted it, and dug through it.

"My parents were not easy people and expected perfection in their son."

Claire didn't speak, just kept her hands in the soil and her eyes on his face.

"I struggled with perfection, so they pushed me harder, and my failures became bigger and bigger as I strived to achieve the goals they set."

Pain was there in his eyes as the memories took him back to his youth. Pushing her fingers deeper, she rested them on top of his.

"The only moments I remember that were happy were the rare times my aunt and uncle visited. They would take me to the garden and teach me the names of plants and flowers."

"What did your parents do to you, Simon? Did they hurt you?"

His laugh was harsh as he turned his palms over and gripped her fingers. "Nothing that caused pain, Claire. They simply locked me in the nursery until I had memorized every task they set me. Sometimes I was to spell. Others, recite Latin. The lists were varied but all were long. I was then to answer their questions as they stood before me, each one directed at me one second after I answered the first. If I failed, they locked me in again until I succeeded."

Dear lord, they may have not hurt him physically, yet they had hurt him. He carried the scars deep inside. She could see it as his shoulders hunched instinctively to protect himself from the memories.

"How old were you?"

"They died when I was a child."

Too young to have suffered at the hands of the people who should have provided his care, loved and protected him.

He turned his hands over once more, releasing her fingers to dig deeper in the soil. Claire couldn't keep still. She had to sift, pat, and smooth, now that she was no longer anchored to him. "You must constantly have dirt under your nails," she said aloud when the silence became uncomfortable. It was a silly thing to say, yet she was nervous in his company. They had spent days together, yet now he seemed like a stranger to her.

"Men like dirt under their nails."

"Some men," she qualified thinking of Lord Pepper and his white hands and neatly shaped nails.

Claire sighed as once again, he fell silent. "I'm sorry, Simon, for getting you into this mess, but it is done, and now we need to discuss how to break our betrothal."

He looked at her, his emotions hidden behind an unreadable expression.

"We will wed."

"You are not thinking clearly, Simon."

"I think the fact that I have slept the past few nights and you have not, qualifies me as the one who is thinking clearly, don't you, Claire?"

Claire knew he had not meant to hurt her by bringing up her own failings, yet he had, because she was tense and yes… tired. Lifting her hands, she shook them briskly. "I have managed to make rational decisions with little sleep before, my lord, I'm sure I can do so again."

"Claire—"

Ignoring him, she stepped off the box. Picking up her gloves, she then walked away leaving him standing there with his hands in the dirt, eyes burning like hot embers into her back.

Claire did not see Simon again that evening. She bathed a reluctant Louis, who had suddenly found his voice and was cursing like a French sailor. She persisted, and finally, a clean little boy emerged.

"Surely you feel better now, Louis, with all that grime washed from your body?" Claire rubbed him dry and then dressed him in the old nightshirt a maid had given her. She wondered if it had belonged to Simon.

"Non."

She laughed at his belligerent expression and then began to brush the tangles from his hair, producing more curses, which, she pointed out gently, were not nice to say at any time. Soon he was clean, and she tucked him into bed. They ate on trays, and Claire sat with him, telling him some of the stories she remembered from her youth until his eyes grew too heavy, and he fell asleep. Tonight they would both miss Simon and his big presence sprawled out below them on the floor.

Her room was next door, so she bathed and pulled on her nightdress, too, and then lay on her bed. There was little chance of any sleep tonight. Memories of her nights spent in Simon's arms made her sad. She would never have them again, so she pushed the thoughts aside and made plans.

She would leave for London early, without anyone knowing, where Claire would then confront her brother. She would tell Mathew of her faux engagement, and how it was her fault entirely that Simon had offered for her. She would then come here and gather up Louis and make their home at her brother's estate. Mathew would not force her from his home. She knew him well enough for that, yet he would never welcome Louis to London, and neither would their mother. Therefore, her life would be in the country from this day forward. She would not wed, nor live in society, and although she would miss her friends, she would not miss many aspects of the life she now led.

She let the thoughts come and go as the hours ticked by until she was sure the household was asleep, only then did Claire leave her bed and pull her shawl around her shoulders. Taking the candle, she made her way to the end of the hall, where Simon's aunt had told her the library was. There was a chill in the air that made her wish for slippers, but if she kept to the rugs, it was not so bad. Studying the books upon reaching the library, she found a section on gardening and smiled, wondering if Simon had read each one. Thinking of him made her chest hurt, so she moved on to the next shelf.

"If I may suggest *Health and Good Will to Your Roses*. I've always found that excellent bedtime reading."

He was leaning against the doorframe, looking rumpled and handsome. However this time, he had thankfully pulled on a shirt, although his large feet were bare and the shirt buttons done up wrong. Claire forced herself to ignore the flutter in her chest and turned to once again look at the books. Drawing in a deep breath, she tried to steady herself before speaking. "Go back to bed, Simon."

"Have you slept at all?"

"Please, go back to bed, Simon," Claire tried again.

"Surely you know by now that I am not good at taking orders, Claire."

She knew he was getting closer because somehow she could feel him. "There is no need for both of us to be tired in the morning, Simon. Besides, I am used to the condition. You are not." Claire made her tone light, when inside, she was suddenly tense and nervous. So much had changed between them today—in the last few days—and now she was uncertain around him.

"Actually, I have already had several hours' sleep."

Surprised, she faced him. "You could sleep with all those thoughts rolling around inside your head?" Claire was jealous. She had often wanted to stop thinking for a few hours—long enough to get some sleep. It seemed the only time she could truly do that was in this man's arms.

"One thing you should know about me, Miss Belmont, is that I can eat and sleep no matter what is rolling around inside my head."

He didn't sound angry anymore, and he was so close now the air around her had suddenly changed, almost as if it was alive with something. "Simon, go back to bed, and we will decide the best course to break our betrothal in the morning."

"I'm sorry I hurt you today. I should not have dismissed your sleeping problems so lightly."

"It matters not, and I was being overly sensitive. You were remembering your youth and were still angry with me over what you've been forced to do."

"I was angry with the circumstances that were forced upon us, Claire, not with you, and I should not have spoken as I did." He moved closer, his bare toes brushing hers. It was the briefest touch, yet she felt as if he had wrapped his hands around her feet and stroked them. "I sometimes need time to sulk and run things through in my head, and I did not get that time until I arrived here. It is childish of me, I know, but unfortunately, I have always been that way."

"Go to bed now, and I will follow soon, Simon."

"Liar."

He leaned forward slowly, and Claire could not pull away. She was mesmerized by the look in his grey eyes. Gone was the emotionless man, and in his place was danger. Heated eyes roamed her face and her body, and Claire felt a sudden hunger sweep through her that robbed the breath from her lungs. "What are you doing, Simon?"

His lips touched her neck, brushing over the skin softly.

"S-Simon."

"I can think of nothing but how you were in my arms that night, Claire." He moved to her chest and kissed the skin with soft touches, stopping when he reached her buttons. His fingers released the first one and then the next. His movements were slow and torturous, and Claire could hear the rasp of her breath as he reached the last button and slipped it through the hole. The breath caught in her throat as he opened the bodice wide, exposing her breasts.

She couldn't speak as he touched her. A long finger traced the outside of one of her breasts as his eyes held hers. She arched toward him as that finger touched the sensitive tip of her nipple. Dear god, that wonderful ache was building between her legs again, that sensual heat mounting inside her once more. He kissed her then, seeking, teasing, and searching out her response, which she willingly gave. His large palm cupped her breast, and she shuddered beneath him. Claire had no idea how long he kissed her for—minutes, hours. She lost every thought but for the man who held her. Where one kiss stopped, another started until finally he pulled back, his breath ragged as he looked at her. Fire blazed in his eyes and was answered in her own as she reached for him again.

"I won't stop this time, Claire."

He pushed her back slowly to the bookshelf, then lifted her hands to wrap around the wood. "Hold the shelf."

She did as he asked, a puppet that was his to control. Her body needed him.

"Sweet Christ, you are beautiful," he rasped before placing his lips on her again. Claire was awash with sensual pleasure as he ran his mouth and tongue over her, caressing each curve and peak, laving and stroking until she was arching toward him, eager for more.

His hands slid beneath the hem of her nightdress, then placing his palms on her skin, he moved the garment slowly up her body. Claire helped him pull it off her head and throw it to the floor behind him.

"Just feel, Claire," he whispered, kissing her ribs. "Focus on the sensations, sweetheart. I want to hear your cry of pleasure."

"Y-your family?"

"Are sleeping and the door is shut."

Closing her eyes, Claire rested her head on the books behind her and felt his mouth on her stomach, kissing the smooth skin and then moving lower. Biting her lip, she fought back the cries she wanted to make.

"Sing for me, sweetheart."

She was an innocent, surely this should horrify her, yet it did not. She delighted in the sensations as Simon taught her body how to respond to his wicked hands and mouth.

"Your scent, Claire—so sweet yet spicy—it drives me wild with need."

His hands parted her thighs, and she felt his hot breath between them. His tongue stroked the soft folds, and his teeth took the small hard bead, and she could do nothing to stop the moan that came from her lips. Her fingers dug into the wood, her knuckles white as he brought her to the brink.

The pressure built and built until she was begging him to release her, and then he once again bit gently into that secret place and pushed his fingers inside her dewy folds, and she was lost. Crying out his name, she shuddered as waves of ecstasy rolled over her.

"Sweet Claire," Simon whispered, regaining his feet.

She knew he was looking at her, but she had no strength to open her eyes. He left her briefly and Claire heard him blow out the candle, and then she was in his arms.

"Simon?"

He brushed another kiss on her lips. "Sssh, Claire. We are safe from detection, and I have your nightdress."

She didn't speak again, just laid her cheek on his chest and let him carry her through the quiet house. Tomorrow there would be questions to answer and futures to discuss, but for now, there was just them.

His door was open, and he walked inside and closed it with his foot. Carrying her to the bed, he lowered her onto the edge and then moved away to pull off his breeches and shirt. He'd left his curtains open, so she could see him as he approached her, see the hard muscled planes of his stomach and long legs. He was the beautiful one, and she wanted to touch him again, feel all that strength in her hands.

Standing, Claire moved toward him, then lifted her hands and placed them on his chest. "I-I want to touch you again, Simon."

He took one of her hands and kissed it. "I want to touch you more."

His fingers stroked her hair as she ran her hands over his chest, and when she leaned forward and placed a hot, open-mouthed kiss just above his heart, the fingers clenched briefly. Moving to his nipples, she circled and sucked, causing the breath to hiss from his lips. She smoothed a hand down his stomach until she felt the jut of his arousal. Trailing her fingers down the rigid length, she caressed him.

"Ah god, Claire, that feels so good." He wrapped her hair around his hands and tugged her head back for a kiss as she stroked him. Soon, he began to thrust against her fingers, and then his hand covered hers and he eased hers free and lifted it to his neck. "I cannot take much more, sweetheart." Leading her back to the bed, he sat on the edge and then urged her to straddle his legs. "Now, Claire, take me inside you."

Claire let him guide her onto his lap, her knees straddling his thighs, and she felt the tip of his arousal push against her.

"There will be pain, sweetheart."

She didn't speak, instead, slowly eased herself down onto him. Claire could feel him stretching her, filling her. She felt Simon's hands on her breasts as he began to caress her again, the sensations stirring her passions. Lowering herself, she felt the sharp stab of pain, and then he was inside her.

"Easy now, love—adjust to me."

His jaw was clenched and his body tense beneath her. Claire knew he was trying to stay still until she was ready to move, and she loved him all the more for thinking of her. Slowly, her body adjusted, so she rose up and lowered herself again, enjoying the feel of him sliding deeper inside her. It was wonderful. It was as if they were one, and the sensations had her doing it again and again. He moaned beneath her, his hands gripping her hips, and suddenly she was lowering as he was thrusting upward, and lord, it was magnificent.

"Claire, Claire." Her name was a chant on Simon's lips as he drove up into her, creating sensation after wonderful sensation inside her. Suddenly, he rolled and placed her beneath him, and she was surrounded by his big body. Her legs wrapped themselves around his hips, and suddenly she felt the wonderful sensations of before begin to build inside her again.

"Let go, Claire—I'll catch you."

She did, and a low, keening sound came from her lips as she scaled the heights of ecstasy once more, and with two more thrusts, Simon followed, then slumped down on top of her. Their limbs were tangled, their bodies, dampened by sweat. Claire kept her arms wrapped around his neck as their hearts thudded against each other.

"Let me go, Claire. I'm too heavy."

She did so reluctantly. He pulled the covers over them and then settled her onto his chest.

"Sleep now. Tomorrow is soon enough to think again."

She felt him relax, and soon, the gentle rhythm of his breathing told her he slept. Of course she would not do the same, she thought as a yawn over took her.

Claire woke as the sun began to rise. Turning her head on the pillow, she looked at Simon for long minutes, committing his handsome face to her memory. He had given her so much already, but last night he had shown her the wonderful things a man and woman could experience. She loved him, of course, and could acknowledge that to herself here in his bed. However, it was now time to set him free.

Slipping from the bed, she pulled on her nightdress and hurried back to her room. She would never regret making love with him, yet in doing so, she had complicated matters more. He was an honorable man, and she had no doubt he felt something for her, especially after what they had shared. However it was not love, and whilst she was once prepared to settle for less, she would not do so now, not knowing she loved Simon. It wasn't a startling revelation. She had simply avoided acknowledging it until last night. However it was because she loved him that she would not allow him to settle for less in his future wife.

Hurrying into her room, she pulled her riding habit and boots from her luggage. The rest would have to stay here until she returned. Once she was dressed, she checked on Louis, who opened his eyes as she entered the room.

Claire knelt beside the bed and ran her hand gently over his head. After his bath, his hair had dried to the exact color of Anthony's. "I must go to London briefly, Louis, and then I will return for you. Simon is here and his aunt and uncle, and they will care for you until I return."

"Come back soon?"

She smiled at his little voice. "Very soon, my darling. Now go back to sleep." She wasted precious seconds until she was sure he slept again before making her way out of the house.

The stables were a small distance away, and she hoped, given the early hour, there was someone awake in there. She kept off the paths where she could, to avoid the noise her boots made on the stones, and did not stop to examine the lovely flowers before her.

A sleepy man greeted her as she entered. Lifting her chin and using her no-nonsense voice, Claire said, "Could I please have a horse saddled at once? I am an experienced rider, therefore your strongest, fastest horse, if you please."

Claire kept her expression cool as the man looked at her.

"Would you be wanting company on this ride, my lady?"

"Oh no, indeed, I will not. I am quite capable of a good morning gallop, thank you."

"The problem is, my lady, we don't have a side saddle on account of no ladies ride here."

Claire felt her stomach plummet to her toes.

"I shall ride astride, then."

He looked briefly at her legs encased in her habit but said nothing further, shrugging he moved to do as she requested.

Soon she was seated on big-boned black horse that looked like he could run all day."

"He's a lovely boy. What is his name?"

"Gus," the man said, nudging her leg forward. He then shortened her stirrups.

"Well then, thank you very much for your assistance, sir, but I must be on my way now." The man stood back and let her leave, and Claire felt him watching her as she walked from the stables. She made her way to the driveway, praying that no one had woken and was looking out the windows. Releasing a loud breath upon reaching the gate undetected, Claire then touched her boots to the flanks of her horse, and it sprang forward. She had ridden astride before, and tucking her skirts securely around her made it comfortable, plus she could ride faster.

She knew what had to be done and knew it was her family that must hear first. Society would no doubt turn their backs on her, but she would make sure Simon's name remained untarnished.

Turning, she blew a kiss at the house in the distance—to the man she loved and the boy who was now hers to cherish. And then, urging Gus forward, she did not look back again.

CHAPTER FIFTEEN

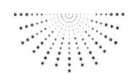

"Where is Claire?"

His aunt and uncle looked up as Simon walked into the room. He had woken smiling and had reached for her, and she hadn't been there. She had also not been in her room or with Louis, who was sitting at the table eating toast slathered in jam, though much of it was smeared on his face.

"I have not seen her this morning, Simon. I had thought because of her ordeal that she may have slept in, and that is why I went to Louis's room to help him wash and dress before bringing him to breakfast. Do you think perhaps she is walking through the gardens?"

"Perhaps, aunt, yet I don't think so." Simon's eyes fell on Louis, who was now watching him intently.

"Do you know where your aunt is, Louis?"

He nodded and then took another bite of his toast. Simon moved to his side and pulled a chair closer so he could look the boy in the eye. He looked rested today. Some of the shadows in his eyes had gone. He knew it would take time for Louis to become comfortable with them and the lifestyle he would now lead. However he believed, given his age and with the love both he and Claire would give the boy, he would adapt.

"Where is she, Louis?"

The little boy thought about his question briefly and then said, "London."

Simon literally shook his head. He hadn't heard that word correctly, surely. Claire would not just leave, especially after what they had shared and not after the way he had spoken to her the last time she had run from him. "Pardon?" he questioned the boy politely.

"London."

Simon felt the color quite literally drain from his face. "Of all the irresponsible, foolish—Pardon me." Simon stopped when his uncle cleared his throat. She'd done it to save him, of course—gone to London alone to confront her brother and break the betrothal, believing he wanted this. If she'd just waited until this morning, he'd planned to tell her he wanted her as his wife, needed her in his life as much as the deep gulp of air he'd just inhaled. Bloody woman! Always charging off without thinking. When he got hold of her, he'd shake her until her teeth rattled. Had she thought last night meant nothing to him? Christ, the thought of her traveling to London with only a coachman for protection made his stomach churn. He wondered how she had coerced one of his drivers to accompany her and prayed it was Merlin. The man would make sure she stayed safe until he reached her.

This time when I catch you, Claire Belmont, I'm keeping a firm hold on you.

"I will need to borrow your carriage, uncle," he said, storming from the room. Running down the stairs, he made for the stables, arriving in minutes.

"She's riding to London on my horse!" he yelled minutes later as he faced Ned, his stable master. Merlin and Ben, he noted, were keeping their distance, both brushing horses and not meeting his eye.

"Said she was experienced, my lord, and in need of a strong horse, as she was a good rider. Thought she was heading out for a gallop and nothing more. I never would have given her a horse, had I known she was riding it to London."

"Merlin, get out here!"

"My lord?" He appeared before Simon in seconds.

"Prepare my carriage at once. That bloody foolish woman has taken it upon herself to ride to London, and she'll be lucky if she reaches it in one piece."

"At once, my lord."

Fear mixed with rage as he ran back to the house. Taking the stairs two at a time, he wondered if even now she was being chased by someone bent on harming her. No, he would help no one, least of all her, with those thoughts. His family was still at the breakfast table, and if possible, Louis had more jam on his face as he re-entered. "I must go to London but will return shortly with Miss Belmont."

Louis slipped from his chair and moved to Simon's side. Surprisingly, the boy then wrapped both arms around one of Simon's legs. Picking him up, Simon held him close, knowing he, too, would now be covered in jam. "It is safer for you here for now, Louis," Simon said gently. "My aunt and uncle will care for you until we return."

"Don't leave me."

God, the look in those eyes nearly dropped Simon to his knees.

"I told Miss Belmont we would care for the boy, Simon, but it seems he does not want to stay with us, nephew, so take him with you." His aunt came around the table with a napkin and proceeded to clean Louis's hands and face.

"I want Aunt."

"My French is not as good as it was, Simon, but I think he said he needs his aunt. Take him to her and then bring them both back soon, darling."

Giving his aunt a kiss, Simon then nodded to his uncle. "I will return as soon as I can, but if it is not in the next few days, I shall send word that all is well."

Simon swung the boy onto his shoulders as he headed outside to his carriage. Merlin sat in the driver's seat while Ben held the door. "As fast as is safe, Merlin, as we have Louis with us," Simon said before climbing inside.

He kept his eyes on the windows as they traveled the short distance to London and prayed Claire had arrived there safely. He'd believed before the trip to Liverpool that his life was complete. Each day was filled with things he liked to do and the occasional one he didn't. He had Eva and Daniel, and they had given him Georgia— what more could he ask for? He'd known there was a wedding in his future, yet he had not been in a hurry to marry. Then Claire had changed everything. He needed her now. She was his future, the woman he loved. She would challenge him, torment him, and make him want to strangle her, but she would love him, too, and at the end of the day, he was the man she'd used as her pillow. God, she'd been magnificent last night, with her lovely body and smooth satin skin. The scent of her had wrapped itself around him and held him tight. She'd not shied from anything he'd done. In fact, she had loved it. Each touch and taste had resulted in delightful little noises that had hiked his passions higher.

"This is London?"

Good god, he was lusting after Claire with her nephew seated beside him. "I thought you were sleeping, Louis," Simon said, brushing aside the hair that tumbled over the boy's forehead as he shook his head. Eager to see everything, the boy stood on the floor between the seats and went from one window to the other.

"You must listen carefully to me now, Louis," Simon said, intercepting him as he made another pass. Lifting him onto his lap, he looked into the boy's eyes. "While we are here in London, you must stay close to me or Aunt Claire, Louis. Do you understand?" The boy nodded and then looked wide-eyed out the window once more. Minutes later, they stopped outside the Belmont townhouse. Simon had wondered if this was the right course of action, bringing the boy here, however, he'd had no other options. Holding Louis in his arms, he knocked on the door.

"Good morning, Lord Kelkirk."

"Plimley." Simon nodded. The man really was too good-looking. Even he felt flustered in his presence. Louis just stared in wonder at the Adonis as he stood aside to let them enter. "We are here to see, Miss Belmont, please."

The butler gave him a gentle smile. "If you will follow me, I will take you to her."

"Before we do, Plimley, can I thank you for caring for Miss Belmont for the years you have known her?" Simon felt someone needed to thank the man for his support of Claire, and as her family did not know of her sleeplessness, he thought it was up to him.

The butler stopped briefly. He didn't turn but gave a deep sigh before nodding his head. "Thank you, my lord, but it has never been a chore."

Interesting, Simon thought, following his very straight back. Did the man have no faults? His voice didn't annoy and his appearance was stunning. Perhaps he had one toe that turned in, or maybe his ears were over large. Moving closer, Simon saw the perfectly shaped ears and dismissed the last. Plimley was not alerting Claire that they were here. In fact, he was taking them right to her, which was another point in the man's favor. He wondered if it was a chore to be so perfect? Simon had certainly never perfected the art. He heard the raised voices then, as they reached a closed door. There was both a male and a female voice, and he guessed the latter belonged to Claire, as he didn't think Lady Belmont could yell like that.

"You are a hypocrite, Mathew. You sit in the House of Lords and work for the poor, bringing attention to the conditions in which they are forced to live and work, yet you cannot even take the time to acknowledge your brother's child."

Definitely Claire, Simon thought.

"You defied me, Claire, and traveled to Liverpool alone. You have brought shame on this family."

Releasing Louis, Simon lowered his feet to the ground.

"Stay with the handsome man now, Louis, and he will take you to the kitchens for some food. All will go well," he added as the boy shot a worried look at the door behind which Claire was arguing with her brother. He couldn't understand what was being said, but he understood the anger behind the words.

"Aunt Claire is all right, Louis. I promise you."

The boy took Plimley's hand then, and the butler led him away.

"I did what you should have done, Mathew. What your responsibility as head of this family should have been." Claire's voice was lower now and she was no longer shrieking at her brother.

"You are a disgrace, sister. No man will have you now, and I demand you leave London at once. I wish never to set eyes on you again!"

Simon opened the door on those words, the handle crashing into the wall as he pushed it wide. No one, not even her brother, spoke to Claire like that. Stalking forward, he passed his now open-mouthed betrothed and grabbed her brother by the shirtfront. "I will have her, Belmont. She is to be my wife, and you had best watch how you speak to her in the future."

"Wife?"

Simon released the man to prevent himself from planting a fist in his face. It would not be a good start to his nuptials if he struck his future brother-in-law.

"Your sister has a heart bigger than any I know. She is brave and beautiful, and you should be bloody worshiping her. She went to collect Louis because he is your brother Anthony's son, Belmont, and she was willing to give up everything in her life just to secure the child's safety. Have you no idea of her worth?"

Before him, Mathew Belmont seemed to wilt before his eyes.

"How dare you treat her so callously? She is worth ten of any lady I know."

"You wish to marry my sister?" Belmont whispered.

"I do, and Louis will live with us." Simon did not look at Claire but heard her sniff. "Would you turn your back on your nephew, Belmont, because he was unfortunate enough to be born out of wedlock? Are you like so many of the others who live among us, a shameful bigot just because you were lucky to be born on the right side of the sheets?"

Ashen now, Mathew looked at his sister.

Simon looked at her, too. Her skin was pale and her eyes over bright. She was close to tears but apparently reluctant to let her brother see her shed them. Her close-fitting riding habit hugged the body he now knew intimately. Her hair was plaited in two long tails, with one sitting higher than the other on her head, which suggested she had done the job herself. She still wore her dirty boots, and to his eyes, she had never looked more beautiful.

"Simon, you should have stayed with Louis and your aunt and uncle. Coming here and saying what you have—"

"We will marry, Claire, so it would be in your interest to get used to the idea, and Louis is with me—in fact he is in your kitchen with Plimley."

"You brought him to London?"

"He would not let me leave without him. He wanted to see his aunt, who, incidentally, I'm bloody furious with. How dare you run from me again?"

"I thought it best—"

"Well, stop thinking," Simon snapped. "It only makes you do idiotic things."

She flew around the desk and into his arms so fast, he stumbled backward several steps.

"Thank you, oh thank you so much for… well, everything."

He held her face in his hands. "We will wed, Claire. I'll have your word."

"But you do not wish it." He saw the vulnerability again, the belief that she was not worthy.

"I wish it with everything inside me, sweetheart," Simon said, kissing her. "Now go and collect your nephew. Your brother and I need to talk."

"Is he really Anthony's child, Claire?" Mathew Belmont sat now, and he looked suddenly a lost man.

"Yes, Mathew, he is."

"Go now, sweetheart. Louis will be scared alone with strangers. Give us a few minutes, and then bring him back to meet his uncle."

"I won't let him hurt him, Simon."

"He's a good man, Claire—you know he is," Simon said, knowing Belmont was listening. He hoped he was right. She nodded, and then he watched as she ran from the room. He walked to the chair on the other side of the desk and sat, giving Belmont a few moments with his thoughts.

Lifting his head, Mathew Belmont stared at him for several seconds before nodding. "I don't understand how you came to be involved in any of this, Kelkirk."

Simon sat forward, looking steadily at Claire's brother. "I intercepted her as she was about to get on the stagecoach for Liverpool."

"Dear god." The man was now whiter than the paper on his desk.

"Precisely."

"What happened to your face?"

"I got these protecting your sister," Simon said, deciding it wouldn't hurt Belmont to hear a few details, even if he modified them slightly.

"Dear god," he said again, however this time it was a hoarse whisper.

"I will marry your sister as soon as can be arranged," Simon said, making sure the man understood his claim on Claire.

"Should I ask why?" Suddenly, Mathew Belmont was a brother. His eyes narrowed as he glared at Simon, who was glad to see evidence of emotion because it meant he cared.

"No."

Neither man looked away until finally Mathew said. "I could not have chosen better for her, Lord Kelkirk. Thank you."

Simon had thought about this conversation on the way to London, and he believed it was time to rid this family of their secrets. Only then would they start to heal the wounds left by their brother's death and the years of misunderstandings and indifference. He hoped Claire would understand why he was doing it and forgive him. Simon knew the importance of family, and deep inside, he suspected Claire did, too.

"Did you know your sister doesn't sleep, Belmont? That she walks these halls for hours until dawn? She has not slept well since Anthony's death."

"Anthony once mentioned it to me. However I did not ask Claire until recently if she still suffered, and she did not give me an answer."

"She rigidly controls everything else in her life because only then can she get through each day."

"How do you know these things?" Once again, his eyes were narrowed, and he had half risen from his chair.

"A little late now for brotherly concern, don't you think, Belmont? And how I found out is not the concern, only that I did."

Belmont sank back into his chair. "She has been looking tired lately."

"Perhaps if you had looked a little further than the end of your nose, you would have seen how much she needed you," Simon snapped.

Simon vowed then and there that he would never treat Claire so carelessly. Their marriage would not be starting under ideal circumstances, but then neither had Eva and Daniel's, and look at them. She would know she had a husband who cared for her, Simon vowed.

"Why didn't she tell me?" Mathew Belmont whispered. "I would have helped her."

"You'll need to ask your sister that, Belmont, because right now I want to discuss our wedding."

LOUIS SMILED as Claire entered the kitchens. He was sitting on a bench and had two maids and Plimley dancing attendance on him, all trying to get him to talk by tempting him with cake.

"Thank you all for looking after Louis."

"Tis our pleasure, Miss Belmont. He's a sweet little boy."

"Thank you, Plimley. Yes he is."

Lifting Louis down, Claire saw the questions in the eyes of the maids and butler, and she knew there would be talk soon. Squaring her shoulders, she took her nephew's hand and made her way back upstairs.

Claire's ride to London had left her muscles aching and her head a mass of turbulent thoughts. She had hoped the time alone would give her clarity, yet she was more conflicted than ever. She loved Simon—there was no doubt in her mind about that—and the thought of marrying him was a dream she knew with only a few words she could put into reality. But did he really wish to marry her? He'd said he did and she wanted to believe him. They needed to talk alone so she could be sure his insistence was not motivated by honor.

"We are seeing Simon?"

"Yes, Louis, we will see Simon." She squeezed his hand gently.

Her interview with Mathew had started well enough, with him showing concern over her early return and asking what had occurred. Then things had steadily grown worse as she'd explained where she had been. Simon had arrived when Mathew had started yelling, and said such wonderful words about her. He believed her heart was bigger than any he knew and that she was brave and beautiful.

Approaching her brother's study, she heard only the rumble of male voices, yet no yelling. Surely that was a good thing? Leading Louis in, she found her brother and Simon seated, conversing with each other over Mathew's desk. Simon rose and came to her as she approached.

"Have you eaten all the food in the kitchens, Louis?"

The boy flashed a small smile and nodded.

"I will surely have to seek employment to keep my pantry stocked, then."

"Dear Christ, he is the image of Anthony as a child, Claire." The words were a hoarse whisper from behind Simon. Claire picked up Louis and held him close.

"Introduce Louis to his uncle, Claire." Simon brushed her cheek with a warm hand as he spoke, and she wanted to lean into him and feel his strength. "He will not hurt either of you, and if he does, I will kill him."

The words were spoken in jest, yet Claire knew if Mathew said or did anything Simon did not like, then he would make the man pay, and it was that knowledge that gave her the strength to leave his side and face her brother.

"Louis, say hello to your uncle."

Mathew came to meet Claire as she moved around the desk. "His eyes are identical." The wonder in Mathew's words mirrored those of Claire's when first she'd met the boy. "It is as if Anthony is here in this room with us."

Louis let Mathew place a hand on his head as her brother came to terms with what was before him. She saw that his fingers shook as he slid them down one soft cheek and cupped Louis's chin. "Will you ever forgive me for my ignorance, Claire? For nearly losing him and the chance to let Anthony's legacy live on in our lives?"

It was the tear that rolled down his cheek that undid her. Her strong brother, the man who seemed to need no one or nothing, was crying. "I only said what I did to protect you and mother. I never truly thought a child existed, Claire. I need you to believe that."

"Mathew, we have a nephew," was all Claire said as she leaned into him with Louis. "He's ours to love, brother, and it is my belief that he has not had much love in his past, so we have much to make up for."

She felt his arms wrap around them, and his cheek rested on top of her head. "I will make it up to you, Claire—to both of you," he vowed.

"There is nothing to make up, Mathew. We start with our future now—today. The past, we leave behind."

She felt his lips in her hair. "Yes, Claire, we start to live today."

Sniffing, Claire stood once more. "He speaks only French, Mathew, so we have much to teach him."

"Hello, Louis," Mathew said in faultless French.

"Hello," Louis replied in his gruff little voice.

"How old is he?"

"Six, we believe," Simon said, coming to her side.

"Will you let your new uncle hold you, Louis?" Claire questioned her nephew.

"Do you have food in your drawers, Belmont?"

Looking puzzled, Mathew went to his drawers and opened one. He found a small twist of paper containing toffee, which Claire knew was his weakness.

"Your uncle has food, Louis." Simon said and laughed as the boy held out his arms toward Mathew. "He has a ferocious appetite."

They watched Mathew hold the boy gently, settling into his chair as he opened the paper and fed the sweets to him one at a time. "You should have told me about your sleep problems, sister."

Claire looked from Simon to Mathew, then back to Simon. "You told him?"

"You should have told him long ago, Claire. This was not a burden you needed to carry alone."

"It was my problem. You had no right to tell him, Simon." Claire said as she felt her old uncertainties rise.

"Why did you not tell your brother, Claire? Did you think it would make you weak in his eyes?" Claire tried to look away from the grey eyes before her, but Simon held her chin. "You are not weak, Claire. You are strong. What you have just done shows that. To heal the divide in your family, there must only be the truth now."

She didn't respond. Was he right? Should she have told Mathew and even her mother?

"You are no longer alone, love. I am here, but so are your family if you reach out to them."

Looking up at him, Claire knew she had to tell him how much she loved him.

"I'm sorry, sister, for your loneliness. I would have stayed awake with you, had you given me the chance." Mathew's words were softly spoken, yet Claire heard them. "You are my sister, Claire, and I have loved you since the day you were born. To my lasting shame, I did not know you were unaware of that fact until now."

"And I, Mathew, love you also."

Claire could see the pride in Simon's eyes as she and Mathew told each other what they should have many years ago. So much emotion rolled around inside her, she had to tell Simon how she felt about him right now, because he was correct, she could no longer hide herself behind the façade that had been Claire Belmont.

"Simon, I'm about to tell you something because I want you to know it, not because I expect you to act on it."

He wrapped one hand around her waist and pulled her slowly closer.

"My brother and nephew are in the room," Claire whispered.

"And are absorbed in each other. However, you had better be quick, as I fear Louis's absorption will stop with the end of your brother's toffee."

"These last few days, Simon, I've come to realize something." Claire felt the words suddenly stick in her throat.

"Just say the words, Claire."

"What words?"

"The words."

Her eyes held his for long seconds. "I don't know how it happened, Simon."

"How what happened?" He knew, she could tell by the sparkle in his eyes, but he was not about to make it easy on her.

"We've known each other for so long, and sometimes we could not even tolerate each other's company."

"In fairness, it was always you who could not tolerate my company," he said.

"I was insufferable, Simon. I'm sorry." Claire realized she had treated him badly over the years, and he deserved an apology from her.

"For the love of god, woman, will you just tell me."

"Tell you what?" Claire said, trying to keep her expression innocent and give him back a bit of what he had given her.

"Claire."

"I love you, Simon, so very much," she said in a rush. "But I will not hold—"

His lips were hard on hers as he stopped her words, and Claire resisted for a second before melting against him. "I love you, too, Claire Belmont, forever and always. Now tell me you will be my wife."

"I'll be your wife, my love, as soon as we can arrange it."

"Tomorrow," he whispered. "I want to wake with you in my arms every morning from that day forth."

Claire gave him that soft smile she had seen Eva give Daniel. The smile that spoke of love and hidden secrets only she and Simon would share for the rest of their lives.

EPILOGUE

"I cannot believe you coerced my butler into your household, Claire."

Laughing, Claire hugged her brother, who returned the gesture freely. "Plimley loves me, Mathew. What can I add to that except the better Belmont won?"

"And I love you, too, sister."

Standing on her toes, Claire kissed his cheek loudly. "And I you, brother."

Releasing him, she walked around the room slowly, making her way to Simon.

A fire blazed in the hearth as outside snow blanketed the ground. This was their first Christmas as husband and wife, surrounded by their family and friends. They were all here. Daniel and Eva had brought Daniel's grandmother who for the most part was behaving herself. Claire's mother and brother were here, as were Simon's aunt and uncle. Louis lay on the floor beside the fire, pulling faces at Georgia, who gurgled back at him. He was a different boy from the solemn one of a few months ago. He laughed and chattered now, and was loved by all who met him. But it was Simon and Claire he turned to when hurt or upset. He was their boy, and Claire knew he would be a wonderful older brother to their children when the time came.

Marriage was a revelation to Claire. Simon wasn't a passive husband. He liked to talk to her, know what she was reading or thinking, and involve her in his day. He laughed loudly, sang off key, kissed and hugged her continuously, no matter where they were, and never since the day he'd declared his love to her had she doubted him. He was quite simply the most wonderful man she had ever known, and his love had changed her. She was now demonstrative. She, too, sang off key and danced with him in the dining parlor or garden if the mood struck. Just looking at him made something inside her go soft, and the feeling of belonging body and soul to another being filled her with joy. She'd existed before he came into her life; now she lived.

"I can tell by the faraway look in your eyes you're thinking about something important, my love. Care to share your thoughts?"

Claire lifted her face for the kiss she knew would follow those words. It was soft and sweet and left her tingling all over. Slipping an arm around his waist, she rested against him. "I was just wondering how I lived each day without you." She felt his lips in her hair as his arms tightened around her. "I existed, Simon, nothing more, before you. It is you that have taught me how to live and love."

"But there you have it wrong, love. It is you that have taught me. I wake each day with you on my chest and wonder how I could have woken alone for so many years. With you, I am the man I want to be, Claire—your husband and Louis's father, but more importantly, the man who loves you to the soles of his large feet."

Claire didn't brush aside her tears as she would have. Simon loved her tears, especially if they were tears of joy. Looking up into his eyes, she smiled at her beautiful man. "Forever and always, my love."

THE END

Printed in Great Britain
by Amazon